He Spoke *After* Ten Years

APURVA MATHUR

INDIA · SINGAPORE · MALAYSIA

To Soni
For making it happen……

1

OCTOBER 31ST, 2023

Mumbai, 11:30 PM

Neel Mantri had finally admitted that someone can be killed for the right reasons. Admitted to himself, of course. Who else? People? Other people? These people? Have you seen them lately? Normal human beings, mere mortals, are generally incompetent, or one can use the word "simple" if one wants to protect their feelings. He was finally convinced that there was definitely something called a rightful termination of life. He was also convinced that life is not actually black or white, and it is not supposed to be that way, either. It is not 0 or 1; it's actually between 0 and 1.

Somewhere.

Sleep eluded the 20-year-old Neel Mantri. Not that sleep was ever welcomed by him, but today, it was not even in the vicinity. Neel was never a fan. He, in fact, hated sleeping, but what he hated the most was that he HAD to sleep… his body demanded it from time to time, and that's why Biology also made it to the top of the hate list. Who wants to be almost dead for 5 to 6 hours and lose precious observation time? … time to observe the world… the crazy beautiful world… the non-binary world… the not just black and white world… the world between 0 and 1. Somewhere.

It was a pleasant Tuesday evening on October 31ˢᵗ, 2023. The youth of Mumbai were out drinking. They were letting their hair down, smoking up, fucking around, and whatever else young juveniles are into. The ODI Men's Cricket World Cup was in full swing, and so was the Indian team. The bars were full every day of the week… people had to compensate for the time lost to the pandemic, and the current buzzing Cricket World Cup was a great catalyst. Tuesday might be a dry day in some households but not in the rest of the city. It was wet and fizzy all around.

Neel ignored the non-stop calls from his friend Gaurang, fondly called "Gau," and one solitary call from his friend/ housemate/childhood buddy, *Shiksha*. He loved Shiksha for understanding him and not calling him for the night out like that idiot Gau. Almost not calling him. This one call was acceptable. He opened WhatsApp and clicked on a group that included him, Gaurang, and Shiksha—The 3 Musketeers. A name he loathed with all his DNA. But it was either this or Three Stooges or Tom, Dick, and Harry. So well… how does it matter? There were no winners here.

Out of 50 incoherent messages, 49 were from Gaurang… and one was from Shiksha. It just said… **"Mood hai toh aaja… Gau is soooo drunk and soooo much fun."**

That's why he loved Shiksha. Lacking unnecessary mush. But he was not going. No way. He knew it. She knew it. She also knew that he would feel bad if that one token invitation call from her did not come. He didn't know that she knew this, but she did. That's why she always called.

He also loved Shiksha for never saying what everybody did… **"Neel Mantri… quit behaving like an old man and start behaving like a young guy, for God's sake… you are 20… 20 years old!!!"** He knew that if anybody could even remotely claim to know him a little bit, it was Shiksha. But she would never claim that, and that is precisely why he loved Shiksha.

Neel walked out of his room into the 400-square-foot semi-covered terrace of this beautiful house he lived in and went to admire one of his most favourite places in the world—THE CORNER.

THE CORNER was a sacred sanctuary to men everywhere. A tall wooden structure with multiple shelves stacked with books and booze. It was a multi-storeyed building, with each storey having either stories from books or stories from booze—all cocooned by mahogany wood. Beautiful. Books and Bar. He was responsible for the enviable collection of books, and the bar was created by his grandfather. Glenlivet, Monkey Shoulder, and Johnnie Walker sat pretty on the works of Harper Lee, William Faulkner, Bukowski, and his current favourite, Jo Nesbo. The works of Ramdhari Singh Dinkar, Ghalib, and Faiz were looking over from the top where they belonged. But his favourite part was at the top right, where The Old Monk stood, the greatest detective writing of Sherlock Holmes by Sir Arthur Conan Doyle and Feluda Mitter by Satyajit Ray.

Classy Corner. Books, Alcohol, and some cigarettes. Just… what's the word… well, there are no words to describe this. Perfection… maybe? It does come close but falls short.

Neel decisively walked up to the corner closet and took out his joint—meticulously rolled. He took out the bottle of Old Monk and poured a generous amount into his rum glass. His grandfather always said…

"Neel… *remember… there is single malt, Scotch, cognac, bourbon, but there will always be Old Monk. On its night… Old Monk can make every other drink look like Laughing Buddhas. And also, when alone with The*

Monk... you are only allowed to play either Jagjit Singh or Pink Floyd... nothing else."

He smiled to himself and thought... Well said, **Amma**!!! As everybody fondly called his grandfather... Amma, short for Anand Mohan Mantri, actually Dr. Anand Mohan Mantri, **PhD and retired Physics Professor.**

There had been many times he felt like a misfit. He did not have any social media accounts. He did not socialise or party. He didn't watch porn but loved to fantasise. Porn was no match for the grandeur and complex storytelling Neel's vivid imagination could bring to sex. He loved women way too much to degrade them by watching or encouraging porn. He loved older women. Full, well-rounded, and intelligent women. It may be a cliché, but he couldn't care less. The music that appealed to his ears was from the 60s and 70s. Language, no bar. Basically, he hated everything contemporary, especially people.

The honest ones called him boring. The sensitive ones called him an old soul. The creative ones called him a 40-year-old man trapped in a 20-year-old boy's body.

Neel's simple logic was that if he found anybody as interesting as him, he would socialise. If he found social media more fun than books, stories, and murder mysteries, he would definitely use it. If the girls his age could ooze even a tenth of the sexuality a mature Indian woman oozes, he would change his preference. So it was not a matter of age; it was all about taste. And right now, this beautiful dark rum tasted amazing.

It was past midnight now, and it was even quieter in his relatively quiet neighbourhood. The rum was drinking quite nicely in this quiet. He was thankful for this quiet, for this silence, which people often discarded for something superior—peace. Neel hated the word "peace" almost as much as he hated the word "passion." But what he hated the most was this current passion for peace. This mad fad of finding oneself and being at peace with it. He hated this blind quest that people were on—to find inner peace. The billion-dollar spirituality industry with influencers having double-digit IQs spewing out bullshit on breathing techniques, yoga, and healthy eating. How predictable can people get, he wondered. Get up at 5 in the morning and go for a walk in a forest, among nature. That pin-drop silence interrupted by sweet chirpings—that is the bliss which eventually leads to your bloody peace. But it's free, so who cares? No one does it.

Ignoring the silence and quiet and running for peace—these people. Always ignoring the necessary in pursuit of the ideal—these people. Fucking people. Silence is local white bread with butter, but peace is gluten-free rye toast with avocado butter. And that's what these fucking people want. People. He almost smirked.

He lit up and took a deep drag on the lung lolly and exhaled the thickest smoke stream with a satisfying and audible exhale. The healthy smoke cloud hung in the aura for a while, dancing with the yellow light. Not white. Yellow light. Dim. Soothing. Private.

And NO!! NO smoke rings. Absolutely NOT!!

He detested smoke rings and hated the people who loved them. That stuff is for wannabes and amateurs and the fucking mouth-breathers this generation is full of.

Smoke rings!!! What's next?

Start smoking those annoying pencil cigarettes or the ones with mint switches. Or worse. You might as well start vaping or have *sheesha*.

Fucking pussies!!!

The audacity of people to infiltrate the sacred world of tobacco with the mint-laced madness of vapes and e-cigarettes. The cold metal dollies barely cater to the nicotine needs of a man. How mechanical! How unromantic! Way to kill the bona fide romance of a man with his silence and solitude, partnered with a cigarette stuck at the corner of his lips.

Fucking Gen alpha, beta, gamma, delta, and their inventions. Keep on inventing and never discover. Typical.

Oh well… the silence. Oh, the silence!!!

No people! No mediocre incoherent mumblings from these wastes-of-space specimens with IQs equal to their age! Just him! and NO people. And Silence. It's not that he never thought about why he detested fellow homo sapiens with such undiminished fervour; he did… constantly. He felt guilty… even sad for himself sometimes, upon his desire to be alone. ***"You are just afraid to be with someone. You have to learn to dislike being alone. It's not healthy," his friends Shiksha and Gau always said.***

"Listen, guys," was his standard reply. ***"I don't want to be bored and be a bore with someone and be unfair to either of us. So let me be, and let me have a good time with myself. Besides, I have you 2, and believe me, I can barely handle you guys and this normal behaviour. You are my prescribed dose of normal."***

He always quipped and irritated his best friends. But he loved them.

He loved them, but he didn't like them. Like is a strong word. Love can be in spirit, but to like is usually in person. And he liked no one. But he loved them. Both of them were responsible for a high-functioning alcoholic like him passing off as a barely functioning social being. He loved them so much that he was constantly mad at himself for being constantly afraid of losing them. He couldn't afford to lose anyone now. So, no people around work… It works like a charm, just like this beautiful joint.

Neel didn't know why he loved this routine so much… Was it because it calmed him and made him happy for the last 3 years, or is it that he still had a couple of days left to turn 21, and this is forbidden pleasure? Twenty-one is the legal drinking age. You want to kill the fun out of something… just make it legal.

It had to be the calm thing… Not happy… Just calm. Happy? He knew he was way too intelligent to be happy. Too brilliant to be happy. Happiness is for simple people and not for superior species like him. That was a bit arrogant, he conceded… narcissistic… maybe. But right… always.

He could feel that his alcohol and joint-induced calmness were being disturbed now, by his own thoughts mostly. He found himself worried and angry again.

The empty glass of rum and the half-smoked joint indicated that his thoughts had found a voice again and were calling him. Neel was fighting hard with his demons.

The flashes of rain, him and his **Maa** driving the car, the song, the hum, her hand. His Maa's hand brushing his hair, her smile, another car, the fear… NOOOOO!

Neel closed his eyes as hard as he could, as if prohibiting any entry to his mind.

Happy thoughts… come on… he said to himself.

Neel got up, went to the corner, and fixed another big drink for himself. He went out in the open and settled himself on the settee overlooking the night sky. He lit the joint again, and it was time to have happy thoughts.

He had to go to his current happy dream. His well-practised, well-rehearsed, happy routine for the last 3 years now, which had never failed to put a smile on his face. He didn't need an audiobook, a podcast, or a motivational video. Yet again, his vivid imagination was more than qualified. It all started when he came across a clip circulating around the advent of COVID-19, which triggered the basic primal warrior instinct in him. His imagination gave him a bespoke dream sequence, which calmed his nerves. Almost instantly.

Neel closed his eyes, relaxed himself, and the dream sequence started.

Neel Mantri. Walking. In slow motion. A little fog was adding to the mystery. Dressed in all black. Black leather pants, black cowboy boots, black leather overcoat, and black cowboy hat. He was going somewhere. Walking with intent. He reached a gate and kicked it open.

It was all black and white with just a splash of red. The red was in his eyes. They were red with anger, desire, and excitement.

Climbing up the stairs. Stealthily. But not afraid. Determined.

The door of the first floor was hurled open. He looked around, looking for him—him... umm... him is too dignified and respectful. So, instead of him, let's call that person the culprit. He walked slowly and looked around. Nothing. He registered a faint noise coming from the top. Terrace. Perfect, he thought. The spooky silence in the background was periodically disturbed as he slowly climbed 2 flights of stairs to reach the terrace. One determined step at a time. The culprit was standing in the corner, admiring the view, listening to music, and smoking.

He lit up an already rolled joint and went on to address the culprit. Tap on the shoulder. The culprit turned around in a flash and then acknowledged the fellow smoker. Took off his earplugs.

"Oh, hey man… what are you smoking?" inquired the culprit.

"Oh, just a bit of weed… quite good it is," he said and took a deep drag.

Long shot. Whitish sky with shades of dark. Two black silhouettes talking on the terrace. Lithium red sunset. Red embers of 2 joints. And when focused upon… his eyes were red. Nice frame.

He took out his phone and played a clip.

"Here, look at this clip. It's quite funny," he offered.

The culprit took the phone and watched with lazy, relaxed eyes. The clip showed the same terrace. Evening time. It showed a guy playing with a 2-month-old puppy. A clueless, cute puppy. The video starts with the guy holding the puppy in his arms and playing with it. And then, in 20 seconds, he was holding the puppy by the tail and swirling it around and… then… suddenly… launched the puppy off the terrace. The puppy was thrown from the fifth floor like a projectile.

Yelp. Thud. Yelp. More yelp.

It could have been louder, but the laughter of the culprit muffled it.

The camera shows the face, and the culprit says, "That was fun."

The culprit, dazed and confused, says, "Where did you find this, bro? That was a fun day."

"Why did you do that?" Neel inquired.

"Why not, man… it's fun! That's what dumb dogs are for," the culprit quipped and took a deep drag.

BANG!!!!

The culprit's kneecap was shattered by the shot fired from Neel's revolver. He was writhing in agony. Yelping. Howling.

"Here… wear this. Quickly and quietly, or else next is your skull." Neel cocked the revolver and threw what seemed like a costume to the culprit.

The culprit, trying hard to breathe and not cry, wore the costume in a flash. One look at the costume, and he knew what was about to happen.

It was a dog suit with all the details. It was the same breed as the puppy in the video clip. There was a dog head, a furry skin coat, and a nice round tail. The culprit started crying for mercy. But the revolver didn't budge.

The culprit was all dressed now. All the detailing of the dog was there except for innocence, purity of the soul, loyalty, and other unimportant things.

"Now dance around and be happy… C'mon," roared Neel.

The culprit with a shattered knee started limping on one leg. And dancing absurdly.

"Now look happy and clueless. Show trust in me. Be around me to make me feel like the most important person in the world. Be defenceless and trusting. C'mon and climb up the wall.

NOW!!!!!"

The culprit climbed up the terrace wall, crying and begging for mercy.

"Shhh… turn around. Face the setting sun. Focus on the view. C'mon."

The culprit closed his eyes in anticipation. A swift kick on the ass, and off he went flying from 5 stories.

Yelp. Thud. Yelp. More yelp.

It would have been louder, but the laughter muffled it.

Neel opened his eyes. He was beaming with happiness. Rightful termination of life. He finished the drink and called it a night.

2

January 19th, 2021

Andheri, Mumbai, 7:30 PM

NO. Absolutely not. He was damn sure he wasn't going crazy. He knew that no one believed him, not even his ever-submissive and docile wife. He was being followed and watched. And it's been a month now. How can he be paranoid in these times? How can he be mistaken when there is no one on the road? It's the goddamn pandemic. There are steps rhythmically following his strut, and callously, too, as if they wanted him to know that… it's time. They… yes… They. It was definitely a group. He got adamant and increased his speed, and they did too. He could tell.

It was the peak of COVID, and there were hardly any souls on the road. The ever-bustling and ever-buzzing Mumbai had come to a grinding halt. It was sad, unbecoming of Mumbai. It looked like a hyperactive, hyper-efficient rave of a city had just run out of cocaine and was coming off a bender in an ugly way. Nobody stepped out unless absolutely necessary. Food, medicine, or alcohol.

He had procured the household essentials just like always and was rushing home. He could bet that this all started a month ago if he was a gambling man. But he wasn't a gambler. He was a man who was sure. Because today, there was a finality in the air. He turned around the last corner and entered the alley leading up to the main road. It was a shortcut he had always taken walking back home. He stopped dead in his tracks when he saw a huge, imposing figure blocking the exit of the alley. He staggered back, and there were 2 figures behind him. He took his face mask off as it was getting difficult to breathe. The figures closed in. Thud. Thud. Thud. Done. Silence.

It all happened very fast. He now lay on the ground with his eyes and mouth half open, as if gaping at what transpired.

He was not crazy.

He was not paranoid.

He was right.

Eknath Patil was dead.

3

November 1ˢᵀ, 2023

Andheri, Mumbai, 11:30 PM

In Mumbai, there is never a special occasion required to enjoy the rain. Every drenched evening presents itself as an opportunity for good times. And if it's an unexpected drizzle that is pleasantly surprising in November, then it definitely calls for a gala time. But today was more than that. Neel Mantri was turning 21 tomorrow, i.e., November 2nd, 2023. It was Neel's birthday, and the gathering was geared towards a surprise party. Gaurang and Shiksha had ensured he stayed away the whole day. It was still half an hour before they were to arrive, and Dr. Anand Mohan Mantri, aka Amma, had ensured that the party was in full swing. Why wait for good times? The venue for the party was the sprawling second-floor terrace of their home, CLARENCE HOUSE, a bungalow made in the epoch of independent India but preserved way better than… well, Independence.

This hidden gem was situated in the hidden Amboli, which was a part of over-exposed Andheri in the belly of ever-awake Mumbai. The second floor was occupied by Amma and Neel; the first floor housed Dr. Ibrahim Sheikh, aka Ibu, and his granddaughter Shiksha. Ibu and Amma were childhood friends and, well, just short of Siamese twins, one would say. On the ground floor lived the person responsible for the well-being and upkeep of the entire household and its inhabitants—Deva. Nobody knew the full name, not even Deva himself. So thus, the mononym was unanimously accepted. Apart from Deva's quarters, the ground floor had a beautiful and blooming vegetable garden and a decent rink with a well-nurtured cricket pitch to practise on. The house gave the feel of a carefully preserved small city ancestral home. Some might say Amma got the deal of a lifetime by scoring this old but spacious bungalow in a building-infested city like Mumbai.

It had been almost 50 years since Dr. Anand Mohan Mantri moved into this house with his late beloved wife, Aarti.

"Almost half a century... 1973, was it?" inquired Prof. Ibrahim Sheikh, aka Ibu, with rehearsed coherence, fully aware of the answer. Ibu and Amma had transcended the word "friends"... they were more like symbiotic existers. No words were required. No communication. Just flawless understanding of each other's minds.

"Yes, yes, it was 1973... the year Pink Floyd released *The Dark Side of the Moon* after a few good ones already... and also came *Daag* with Rajesh Khanna, *Abhimaan* with Amitabh-Jaya, and *Bobby* with Rishi-Dimple... what a year!!!" said Amma, as he was fondly called... a poor, inaccurate, but beloved acronym of his name.

"Life may be measured in moments, but my favourite unit of memory is years, you see... Kamble," said Amma, emptying the first Old Monk bottle of the night. "I tell you... 1973 was the best."

Rachit Kamble, or better, Senior Police Detective Rachit Kamble, was Amma's favourite student. His disciple. Kamble was a typical middle-aged cop, which meant receding hairline, exceeding waistline, and an eye for minute details. They say that once you enter a profession, the profession enters you at the same time. A cop's life is no party. One has to deal with literal low-lifers all the time. It is a pressure cooker with no release valve. So Kamble cherished his time with Amma and his coterie. It kept him sane, normal. The fact that he adored and loved his guru with unconditional devotion just made every sitting memorable.

Amma loved his life, or maybe he just loved life. His house, his alcohol, his friends, and most of all, his grandson—Neel. He was actually grateful for Ibrahim and his granddaughter Shiksha, his house manager for 50 years, Deva, Rachit Kamble, his favourite student, but mostly for Neel. Life was not easy, but it was particularly hard for Neel, he thought. Neel had been called a lot of things—genius, prodigy, arrogant, narcissist, old soul, fake… but Amma knew who he really was. He was hurt. He was broken. He was scared. And Amma was determined to heal him as much as he could in his remaining time on this Earth.

Ibu sensed the train of thought Amma had boarded. He got up, fetched another bottle of the Monk, and unscrewed it animatedly. As he made Amma's drink, he winked at Kamble, who in turn asked Deva to get the pakoras faster and sit down.

Kamble inquired, "So Amma. Neel just stopped talking, huh?" He knew this was sufficient. Everybody knew what Kamble had unleashed. Amma's favourite subject—Neel. But one had to admit. Neel was worth studying.

Amma took his drink from Ibu, acknowledging it with a familiar smile, clearing his throat, and surveying the mehfil. Ibu, Kamble, and Deva hurried down with a plate of spicy, hot pakoras. He picked up a paneer pakora… juggled it… broke it… took a generous dollop of mint chutney, and ate it despite audible warnings from Deva. He let the morsel dance around in his mouth, chewing it while whistling, and gestured to all 3 of them to calm down.

"He was always a very bright and inquisitive child, my Neel. Learnt to speak early, and not just speak. He learnt to pronounce flawlessly and make compound sentences by the time he wasn't even 4! He used to read Sherlock Holmes for an hour every night before bed. One time, I remember, he was doing a jigsaw puzzle, which looked very old, but I had not seen it before. When I asked him why the puzzle looked wrong and didn't make any sense, although all the nooks and crannies were fitting together, do you know what he did?"

Amma took a big gulp and continued… "He asked me to peep from under the dining table glass, and I found that he was doing the puzzle upside down!" Amma let out a loud chuckle.

He put the empty glass down, and Deva tried to get up for a refill. Amma gestured for him not to. At least, not right now.

Amma's expression turned a bit sombre as the memory hit.

"Everything changed that night. My world was turned upside down in a flash, just like the jigsaw puzzle Neel was doing, except nothing made sense, and no nooks and crannies fit… till today. That bright, beautiful boy… my boy Neel lost his mother in that car accident and his father to shock and trauma the same night and was so mad at the world that he just refused to say anything." Amma stopped and kept staring into the sky, holding back tears.

Nobody said anything. Even though everyone knew the story, it choked everyone up every time. That is why Neel was loved by this group of people one can call family.

Amma continued, "It was as if he was mad at the world, everyone, for taking his Maa away. It was a child saying to the world, whomsoever it may concern – ***Main aapse katti hoon aur main ab aapse kabhi baat nahi karoonga.***"

"That boy who had so much to say… who could say it flawlessly even in compound sentences… just refused to talk. I took him to doctors and therapists and whatnot… he would listen to all of them intently… nod yes or no… but not talk. One of the doctors started yelling and threatening him just to shake him… do you know what he did? He gave me a piece of paper on which it said, 'Amma, I am fine. Please stop this.' I took him home and never tried anything again. 10 years went by… 10 years!!!"

Amma was now sobbing and choked up. Deva just got up, gave him a napkin, and quietly took back his seat. Kamble and Ibu knew this but were still overwhelmed by emotion. After a minute, Amma said,

"He never demanded anything he wanted to eat – to me… to Deva… never. He used to read 3 books a week… 3!! But every night before bed, it was either Sherlock Holmes or Feluda Mitter. He would read Faulkner in the morning and Faiz in the evening, Dickens in the morning and Dinkar in the evening. He read and wrote all day. He wrote the letter we submitted to the school principal about allowing him to function without asking him to talk. He put forward a convincing narrative of Post-Traumatic Stress that no one could refute. He detested company. Boys his age were playing cricket and football, eating fast food, and running around all the time. He detested them even more on seeing this."

Amma paused, either trying to recall the incident or just reminiscing about the old days.

"One day, I asked him why he avoided other kids. He said… sorry… he wrote that all the other kids were stupid and not worthy of his time. Can you imagine? Not worthy!! What a pompous ass of a kid!"

Amma was strangely proud.

"Growing up, he had no company. Only books. No friends. No one except my angel – Shiksha." Amma sighed.

Ibu picked up the cue, "Amma named my granddaughter Shiksha against my wishes. I wanted Noor, and my son wanted to name her Roohi, but my daughter-in-law just heard Amma's choice and said, 'That's it…. Everyone, meet Shiksha Sheikh.' What a secular, tongue-twister of an alliterative name… Hahahah… You know, I sometimes feel Shiksha understands Neel more than anyone, I think."

The whole group laughed out loud, and one could feel the love everyone had for the kids—Neel and Shiksha. Ibu took a big gulp of his drink and continued.

"I still remember when we moved here into CLARENCE HOUSE after… umm… the incident. The idea was that Amma and I would be closer and take care of Neel together. Shiksha was supposed to go to the Gulf with her parents, but the day she saw this house, she refused to leave. Her mother couldn't believe that her daughter wanted to live without them, but Shiksha put her cute foot down. When she met Neel for the first time, I asked her what she thought. She said, 'Ibu, I really like him. He is quiet, cute, and very interesting.'" Chuckles everywhere, especially from Deva, and why not? His Neel Baba is all that and more.

"When I asked, 'How can he be interesting if he doesn't even talk?' she replied, 'Ibu, one doesn't need to talk to communicate, you know,' and then she left with my jaw all over the floor." A round of applause followed.

Kamble got up and went to the bar for a refill. He requested Deva to get some ice. While unscrewing the bottle, he continued gleefully, "So then what happened that day, Amma… you know… the day!" Kamble did air quotes with one hand as the other was occupied with serving everyone a generous encore.

Amma took the drink from Kamble's hand and gave him a smile of appreciation.

"It was drizzling just like today, I remember. Ibu and Shiksha were in the Middle East visiting her parents, and Deva had gone to his village, I believe. I was alone and was drinking and enjoying music, making the most of the weather but alone. Neel had turned 18 a week back. So he just came, sat next to me, and poured himself a drink. I said, 'That's illegal, Neel,' and laughed. He meticulously made a Monk for himself, raised his glass to me, and we clinked. I was smiling ear to ear at my boy. He took a long swig, looked at the glass intently, and said, 'Now I see what the fuss is all about, Amma. It's beautiful,' and then he just sat there drinking with me. I was shocked and shaking, I think. I simpered, 'Neel… did you just… talk?'"

"Oh yes, Amma. I think it's time to talk now. Can we please not be dramatic about it now?" Then he finished his drink and left.

"I just sat there all night… drinking… crying… smiling… bawling my heart out and thanking all the Gods there were," said Amma chokingly.

"That son of a bitch stopped talking and started again. All on his own whims," he added.

"Just like that," Kamble mused. "But it is not surprising, Amma… he is cut from different cloth. That boy just knows everything because he wants to know everything. Remember how he used to listen to all the case memoirs I used to share with you? A 12- or 13-year-old boy listening all night to me talking about murders with Amma. Just sitting and listening. And how sharp he is—that I got to know the day he broke open the case of the Antop Hill murder."

Ibu asked quizzically, "Which one was the Antop Hill murder?"

Kamble put down the drink to put on a show. "December 2015. A gruesome multiple murder. Husband and 3 kids dead. Their wife was almost dead when they found her. No clues. No forced entry. No CCTV footage signifying any intruder. Post-mortem suggested poison in the dinner soup. No empty sachets, box, no evidence suggesting who poisoned the soup."

Kamble took a sip and continued.

"The survivor, the wife, the mother, was inconsolable. She tried to kill herself in the hospital, you know. She cut her wrist with the small knife that came with the hospital food. Terrible mood swings. Understandable… right? We were clueless."

Kamble's expression changed to excitement now because he was still amazed at what happened that night.

"I remember one night coming straight to Amma with case files and showing him all the photographic evidence, case files. I ranted for 4 straight hours, and Amma was clueless, too. Neel, who was just listening intently, sat for an hour more, looking at the photographs and pointing at one of the pictures. There were empty soup bowls in the sink, and clearly, one was half-eaten with a smaller spoon. Neel just wrote something on paper which said, **'It's the mother.**

She is the one.' We checked the DNA report, and the soup bowl was hers, which we had brushed off as one of the kids' bowls. The mother!… Can you imagine? It turned out she had been having an affair with a neighbour for many years, and he had moved to Australia just 6 months back." She carefully studied the dosage. She cut her wrist strategically while in the hospital. She had the intention of claiming the insurance money and eventually flying out of India."

Kamble emptied his drink in excitement, inviting a gesture from Amma to slow down.

"Anyway, I asked Neel how he figured that out… he just smiled, pointed at the Sherlock painting in the corner, and left." Kamble mimicked what Neel must have done in a dramatic fashion, his mouth gaping open.

"Amma translated it for me… *'If you remove everything impossible, then whatever remains, however improbable, must be the truth.'"*

Suddenly, Ibu's phone buzzed. He checked and announced, "It's Shiksha; they are here. C'mon, c'mon…"

Deva rushed to the kitchen, got the cake with candles, and quickly lit them. Neel entered the terrace, and everybody yelled… "SURPRISEEE!!!!"

Neel just looked at everyone and the cake and broke into a smile. Shiksha came close to him and whispered softly, "Now c'mon, I know that you knew. Now be nice, OK?"

Neel nodded and entered the party, reluctantly hugging everyone. Gau straight away went to touch everybody's feet, rubbed his hands in excitement, and said… "So…????"

Kamble gave a frosty look to Gau, "Are you 21?" Gau nodded from left to right nervously.

Kamble burst out laughing and said, "*Arey* Gaurang, you are a cutie… come, I will fix you all a drink."

Deva was waiting for his turn. He just put his hand on Neel's head and kissed it. Neel touched his feet, and they hugged for what felt like an endless amount of time. Time stood still. Everybody was fighting tears.

"Someday, he will hug me like that, maybe. I will wait," Amma said wryly, shaking his head and wiping his eyes.

"Me too," Shiksha muttered under her breath. Nobody heard. Nobody had to. Everybody knew. They just did.

Everybody sat down with their drinks. The lights were dim. The weather was cool. And Amma was drunk. So Amma did what Amma did best. He sang.

Chura Liya Hai Tumne Jo Dil Ko...

Everybody was humming and singing together. Even Neel. Amma was air-guitaring while performing his soulful rendition of this classic. He finished with a flourish and a salutation to the semi-drunk audience.

"Long live RD Burman!" hailed Amma.

Kamble suddenly uttered out of turn, "RD Burman these days only reminds me of this case, which has made my life hell. That is not the memory I want RD to invoke... I..." He realised that no one was listening. Except Neel. He continued, "Long live RD Burman!!"

After drinks, food, and cake, the party was coming to an end. Kamble, visibly and audibly tipsy, suddenly turned and said, "Okay, Neel... one for the road. Surprise me... astound us with your sharp observation. Pray tell something interesting and blow our minds... C'mon, do the Neel..."

Neel looked at Kamble intently and turned his gaze to Shiksha. With a slight tilt of the head, he asked her. And with a slight shrug of both shoulders, she replied.

Neel took the bait, "OK... when is Rashmi Kaki coming back, Kaka? It's been more than a week now!"

Kamble became alert and visibly stunned. "How did… Who did… Nobody knows… I didn't even tell Amma… How… and how the hell do you know it's been more than a week…???"

"Are you sure, Kaka? It's embarrassing," Neel warned with a smile.

"Oh, c'mon, I can take it… shoot."

"In the last 2 hours, you have been adjusting your underwear constantly because it is riding up your butt crack. You own 7 pairs of underwear in 7 different colours that everybody knows because you have shared this proudly on many occasions. But today, you have frequent wedgies, which means you are wearing an old pair from when you were… umm… a little fitter. God knows that you will not wash them on your own, and Rashmi Kaki will never let it come to that point. Hence, she is away, and it's been more than a week," Neel signed off.

Kamble turned red, almost bowed to everyone, and left red-faced. Amma, Abu, Deva, and Gau burst out laughing and started winding things up. Neel made one last drink for himself, smiling, while Shiksha was just lost in her thoughts.

4.

November 2ND, 2023

Terrace, Clarence House, 2:00 AM

Everybody had retired: a totally tipsy Gaurang, fire-faced Kamble, Amma, and Ibu. Deva and Shiksha were sorting out the site of another legendary party at Clarence House. Neel was standing in one corner, staring into nothing. He glanced at Shiksha; their eyes met, and something was communicated and understood almost simultaneously.

"It's done, Deva. You can call it a night now. I'll finish this," said Shiksha, finishing up the request with finality. "Please… good night." Deva patted her head and left. She turned around and gave Neel a playful nod. Neel fished out a cigarette and lit it immediately. He took the first drag and exhaled with a dramatic sigh.

"Say thank you, spoilt brat," Shiksha elbowed Neel.

"Ouch… Thank you. Thank you. You want a drag?"

"Yes, actually…" She accepted the cigarette from Neel and took a deep drag. Expertly. And let out a healthy smoke cloud. Without coughing. Expertly.

"Shit, man… You're a natural and a show-off. Ideal combination. I like it," grinned Neel while accepting the cigarette back.

Neel finished and stubbed the cigarette out on the terrace corner. He walked over to where Shiksha was standing and stood next to her, gazing at the same starry spot.

"Thank you, Shiksha. That was a beautiful party. Perfect. Just right. Had there been one more homo sapien more…" They both laughed. He held her hand. He turned her around, and they were face to face. And then, just like that, Neel hugged Shiksha. Shiksha melted in his arms. Happy. Secure. Grateful. Trying hard not to cry. But she lost. With watery eyes, she planted a kiss on Neel's cheek and made a motion to call it a night.

"Happy birthday, Neel. Nighty night," she signed off.

Just before going down the stairs, she announced without looking back, "And don't drink and smoke too much."

Neel, smiling ear to ear, went to the corner and fixed himself a drink. He went to his room and stood in front of the mirror.

"Happy birthday, Neel Mantri and Sir Shahrukh Khan."

There wasn't a single poster of Shahrukh Khan in Neel's room because he wasn't a fan—he was more. He related most to 2 people in his life: Sherlock Holmes and Shahrukh Khan. And no, he wasn't a fan. He was a fellow who understood them clearly, more like a friend. He understood what both of them said, did, and, most importantly, thought. He understood them.

"The party must be in full swing in MANNAT right now, Mr. Khan. But just to let you know, yours truly has turned 21. So for my… OUR next birthday, we'll raise glasses together. I am proud of you, Shahrukh, and I know you are proud of me. Happy birthday again. 21, huh… This is going to be a life-changing year, Neel Mantri. Happy birthday."

Neel finished the glass. Bottoms up. Took off his trousers. Bottoms off. And then almost crashed into bed. Almost hitting his head in the process. Almost half asleep already. Almost smiling.

And just like that… Neel Mantri was 21 now.

5

AUGUST 15ᵀᴴ, 1958

Aurangabad

He was just 9 years old. Timid. Physically weak. Mentally weaker. Scared all the time.

It was a time when India was teething with post-independence problems. If you think there is a huge gap between the metropolitan and Tier II and III cities now, you cannot even fathom the delta 65 years ago. Rural India was not independent in 1958; let's just put it that way. It had its own system, the most popular one—the caste system.

Anyway, he was just walking to school, minding his own business, when he was suddenly hit really hard by a slipper. The blow was not that hard, but he was just that weak. He fell down and started sobbing almost instantly. He didn't even bother to look and inquire how and why it happened, thereby acting as if he deserved it. His sobs were drowned out by the roaring laughter of 5 well-fed kids of the same age but with the opposite demeanour. They were standing right in front, towering over him.

Rubbing his temple, avoiding eye contact, he attempted to circumvent the group to resume his school-bound journey and, as expected, was denied permission.

"What is the point of you going to school when all you have to do is serve us eventually?" roared one of the big guys, the quasi-leader of the group, it appeared. Right on cue, there was loud laughter from the rest of the crew. It looked like that was their job, to somehow perpetuate and maybe amplify their leader's disdain for the disenfranchised poor.

"I suggest you start eating more and exercising more, become stronger. This will help you serve us eventually. Of what use are you with this **bhindi**-like body?" Collective roar.

"C'mon. Turn around. You've learnt the lesson. Turn around. C'mon." Collective judgement and instruction followed by loud, comical laughter and high-fives.

The weak boy was standing there crying. Frozen. And a voice boomed.

"Leave him alone. First and last warning."

Everyone just turned their heads in the relevant direction. Standing there was another scrawny kid of the same age, height, and size, perhaps even weaker. The bullies digested what had just happened and laughed out loud. They pushed the original weak kid to the ground and collectively turned their attention to the scrawny announcer. They started walking towards the scrawny kid with the intent to hurt him, their faces gleaming with derision and contempt. The scrawny kid stood his ground and didn't budge an inch. They were a little surprised, and so was the original weak victim lying on the ground, still sobbing.

"What did you say... say it again..." boomed the bully leader.

"I said... leave him alone... first and last warni..." THAAAAAAAAD. He couldn't finish. The bully hit him with his backhand. The scrawny kid's lip got busted, and blood was trickling down. He got up, wiped his lips with the back of his hand, and, without wasting any time, shouted…

"BALRAAAAAAM PANDIT Haaazir Hooooo!!!!!!!"

On cue, a kid double the size of the bully leader came running from a nearby house. With unbelievable agility, he hoisted himself into the air and jumped on the whole group, taking all 5 of them down together. Then, in the most efficient language of bully justice, he sat on the chest of a bully and slapped him hard 4 times—twice on each cheek. The crew kept watching, frozen. Nobody moved for a second. The bully's face was red and swollen, his lip was bleeding, and then the bawling started. Howling at the top of his voice, the bully and his gang ran off, never to be seen again.

The scrawny kid held out his hand to help up the original victim.

"Don't worry. They will never trouble you again. Ever. My name is Ibrahim Sheikh. They call me Ibu. And this is my friend… Balraam Pandit."

"Hi… thank you so much. My name is Anand Mohan Mantri."

"That's a long-ass name… Anand Mohan Mantri. We'll just call you Amma from today, and you can call me Ibu."

The scrawny duo looked at their beefed-up saviour for a moment.

"I am Balraam Pandit. That's it. Any problem?"

6

November 2ND, 2023

Clarence House, 7:30 AM

The mornings at CLARENCE HOUSE almost had a military discipline in some regard. Deva, the household in charge, was an early riser. No matter how late the party wound up the previous night, Deva was up at 5. The Neel birthday bash went on until almost 2 AM, but precisely at 5:15, Deva was standing in his vegetable garden to till and tend. This was his happy time and happy place. He didn't care for any morning tea or coffee. It was just his tilling tool, Khurpi, and he was in the garden all morning.

Shiksha got up at 6 and loved her own *subah ki chai.* Ibu and Amma had sugar-free chai with tulsi. Deva had a cup full of sugar with a little chai in it. She had adrak-kalimirch chai with normal sugar. Neel had a black coffee. No cream. No sugar. Just coffee. Just black.

Deva loved Shiksha for her morning ritual. Four types of beverages for the entire house of 5, but she always did it. Happily.

It was 7:30 AM. Amma and Ibu were still sleeping. The black rum, which had been consumed extravagantly the night before, was going to ask questions in the morning. Shiksha knew that. So, she fixed chai for Deva and herself and put a pot of fresh coffee for Neel. She went down to the garden with Deva's cup. She loved the morning misty smell of flora.

"Here… Deva!" She extended the steaming cup towards Deva, who was squatted in the corner weeding out the unwanted shrubbery from his proud potato crop.

"Arey… thank you, Shiksha… thank you." His face beamed with genuine affection and gratitude for the girl. He was about to sip his sugar-laden chai and was suddenly interrupted by her.

"Deva…?" She gave a mock expression with a hand on her hip.

"Oh. Oh… *jeeti raho*… hahahha…" Deva patted her head gently and was smiling from ear to ear.

"Now, that's more like it!" Shiksha turned on her heel and ran up to the first floor to collect her chai and Neel's coffee. Stupid Neel. Stupidly cute Neel, she thought.

Shiksha didn't need to knock on Neel's door before entering, ever. She had seen it all. His drinking, smoking, morning glory unadjusted and adjusted both. Out of the 2 of them, certainly, Neel couldn't care less, but surprisingly, she didn't either.

Shiksha entered the room, and Neel was sleeping on his side, only in his underwear, facing the door—and her now. She glanced at his lean frame, slightly unkempt and curly hair, and the scar on his forehead, reminding him of the accident that took his mom. Why did she love him so much?

Why didn't he bother her with what he thought… almost?

Why was she not bothered by his careless nudity? It was seemingly ungentlemanly behaviour.

I guess because it was careless, that's why. The respect Neel had for her… for women in general… was just beautifully endearing.

He once said, "Women are so superior, you know, Shiksha, that they rule the world and are so secure that they let the men believe otherwise. True power lies in anonymity."

Neel was the purest soul that ever walked the Earth. This was true; she knew. She loved his soul so much that the hurt and pain in it bothered her. She wanted to heal him with her love. She knew Neel so well that she knew he would never hurt her; he was incapable, and this very feeling just gave her strength and security.

"Are you done checking me out, pervert?… It's been 5 minutes of your leering!" said Neel, while covering himself up.

Shiksha hurried to the bed and threw a pillow at his head, blissfully unaware that she was blushing pink.

"Listen, Tarzan… I wasn't… Hello… Aaaand just FYI… I was not leering… and certainly not for 5 minutes." Shiksha threw his shorts and vest at him—his favourite white sleeveless loose-fitted vest with just a thick black moustache on it. And the shorts were, well, just shorts.

Neel got up, still in his underwear with the contours of his anatomy showing, making not the slightest effort to hide, and Shiksha was not in the least embarrassed.

"Not leering… huh… Why don't you tell that to your cheeks, which are defiantly pink right now?"

Shiksha turned her face away, thinking that she was really blushing—damn this boy!

"Happy birthday again, idiot," Shiksha changed the topic at once.

He buttoned his shorts and, in one swift motion, put on his vest, picked up the coffee cup, and continued, "Look at this thin and dying steam from the coffee, my dear Shiksha; it certainly has been 5 minutes." And then he let out a chuckle as he sipped his cuppa Joe.

"Chal… let's go to the terrace." And he wasn't asking.

The terrace still bore witness to the **mehfil** that was last night. Empty bottles stacked neatly, haphazard cushions on haphazard furniture.

Neel and Shiksha quick-fixed the **deewan**, or settee, and parked themselves to enjoy their respective brews.

Neel raised his coffee mug to Shiksha and said, "It's perfect… Cheers!"

"Lately, there has been a lot of 'cheers' from you, Neel. Maybe I have no right to say this to you, but please slow down." Shiksha took another sip of her chai so that she would stop talking.

"Yes… yes… I am aware that I have been boozing it up lately, but that's about to change. I have a feeling that I am going to be consumed by something very big. Big enough. Almost deserving of my undivided attention. Well, almost. I can feel it." Neel was pointing at his head while saying this because that's where the feeling is—not the heart, but the head.

"About time… you have not been reading lately, as if waiting for something big, and you have celebrated this anticipation period like how!" Shiksha rolled her eyes.

"Wow… an eye roll this early in the morning! Great start… but trust me. It is coming, and I have a feeling that what Kamble Kaka was sharing yesterday, or was about to share, is going to get bigger. It was strange—not what he was saying, but that he never mentioned a case unless he was lost. Remember something after Amma sang about RD Burman being a bad trigger? He actually wanted to share more, but he didn't because it was my birthday. But he was uneasy, I could see." Neel finished his coffee with precision.

"Oh, he was uneasy, huh… but wasn't that because of his old underwear!!" Shiksha burst out with laughter before she could even finish the sentence.

"Ha ha… oh, that was physical unease… I'm just pointing out his premature sharing… Anyway, we shall soon know." Neel smiled wryly, lost in thought, and when he was, he always clasped his hands together, making an A with his index fingers and placing them under his chin.

She loved that A. He looked cute when he did that. Suddenly, her leering was interrupted by a loud "Shikshaaaaaaaaa…" That was Amma. Cranky Amma. Hungover Amma. And worse was that soon Ibu would follow.

She had to douse the morning ire with Nimbu-Paani followed by their chai. She got up and started walking away from Neel when she heard it.

"You are wrong, Shiksha."

"About what…?"

"You have every right to say anything to me. Every right." Neel announced, still lost in space with an A made out of his hands.

This time, Shiksha was smiling, blushing, and leering. She just wanted to run to him and kiss him, but she didn't. Maybe later, she thought, and proceeded to douse the ire of 2 under-slept, over-aged, and over-enthusiastic drinkers.

Amma and Ibu were sitting at the dining table with quiet guilt. Shiksha came and gave them nimbu-paani without saying a word. She went straight to the kitchen to help Deva fix their chai. Both hungover oldies gulped down the nimbu potion and were thanking the Gods who made lemons and, well… Shiksha. Ten restless minutes passed. Shiksha entered with 2 hot cups of chai, slammed them on the table, and was about to leave when Amma held her hand.

"Oh, c'mon, Shiksha… sorry, yaar. It's the Cricket World Cup. How can we break our routine, **bachchey**?"

"Amma… you are super flexible in life, especially with your diet and exercise. The only non-negotiable routine and discipline is there when it comes to cricket and alcohol," retorted Shiksha.

She continued, "And you. You are the worst… your sugar is playing a high-scoring ODI match every day, but you have to drink, not walk, not diet, eat naan… very nice. Both of you are worse than teenagers."

Ibu was about to say something, but Amma gestured for him not to. He stood up and went face to face with Shiksha.

"Fair enough, bachchey. How about we earn our drinks, huh?… listen… the way India is playing in the World Cup… we are going all the way to the finals and lifting the cup, right? And that is 2 and a half weeks from now."

Shiksha was calm, and that encouraged Amma. He continued, "How about Ibu and I have our rituals on match days followed by an after-party at our mehfil catered by you………" He was interrupted as Shiksha jolted up and said, "Nice booze calendar… not just a party… even an after-party… very nice, Amma…" She was about to storm out but was intercepted by Ibu, who pleaded, "Let Amma finish, beta."

Amma started talking animatedly as if involved in an elevator pitch with a ruthless VC.

"Five. Only 5 more matches to go. We will only make merry on those 5 days. Rest all days are dry. Every day, Ibu and I will walk 10,000 steps. No desserts for a month. No deep-fried stuff either. If we don't follow a single thing, cut us out," Amma finished with his hand stretched out for a handshake.

"Ok… deal. But after we win the World Cup, no drinks till New Year's Eve," added Shiksha.

Amma looked at Ibu, who could barely manage a shrug. "Deal," conceded Amma.

"Now, let's enjoy the chai," chuckled Ibu.

"Let's go for a long walk, Ibu, before breakfast. We play Sri Lanka today," said Amma, taking a sip.

"Whaaaaaaaaaaaat… No, no, no… no party today. The deal starts with the next match," fumed Shiksha.

"Oh, c'mon… yesterday was Neel's birthday. Completely different thing. Besides, you shook on it, Shiksha… ha ha ha… no backsies…" Amma finished the chai.

"Look at you old men, even willing to go for a long walk for the possibility of drinks. Unbelievable."

Amma winked at Shiksha and left while Ibu said, "Men are simple, beta. I always tell you."

7

November 2nd, 2023

Balli's Bar, Mumbai, 6:00 PM

Balli Bhau was the eponymous owner of Balli's Bar. The quintessential cesspool of diehard, sweaty cricket fans in Andheri West, located near the Kabootar Chowk. The simple name of the bar mirrored its simple objective. You love cricket. You love the Indian team. Welcome. Watch. Drink. Cheer. Repeat. If you want to get rowdy—enter Balli Bhau. The 73-year-old owner/founder of the bar. He is 6 foot 3 inches, quiet, has a moustache, muscle mass, and melancholy. A cocktail you absolutely don't wanna taste. A gentle giant, unless poked, who seldom interacted with anyone except the fellow septuagenarians Amma and Ibu.

Balli Bhau used to sit on his elevated throne behind the counter to scan the proceedings.

The regular patrons of this watering hole were settled in their seats like ideal frontbenchers. The Sri Lankan chase was just about to begin. Amma and Ibu were en route.

Balli Bhau was the owner/founder, but his son, Asif, was the chief operating officer of the establishment. He was the reason behind the rustic, testosterone-themed—and mighty successful—Balli's Bar. An unassuming, submissive little semi-open-air ground floor watering hole near the

Kabootar Chowk of Lokhandwala, aptly named. It seemed like a lazy and mediocre attempt to make it sound simplistic, but it was not. One look at Asif made it absolutely clear that it was just what it was. It was a good old watering hole with cane furniture, undiluted honest alcohol, and beautiful music from the early '60s to early '90s—Classic Rock. Loyal patrons. And a mint-condition LP record player with over 1,000 vinyl records stacked up in the almirahs next to it. Dim lights. Open-air and smoke-friendly. Great finger food, especially the fish fingers made with Bombay Duck, crunchy calamari, and a mean garlic coriander dip. And, of course, the soul of it all—sports, especially cricket. Indian Cricket.

"Overnight hung curd, my friend. Good things in life are mostly simple; everything else is just cinema." This was Asif's standard reply when asked about the secret recipe of the mouth-watering garlic dip, laden with unsolicited advice about life.

Asif was a well-preserved 40-something-year-old who inherited his father's millions sans the arrogance, muscle mass, and wandering eye. His was a svelte, thin, athletic frame with a generous amount of salt and pepper splattered on his head and face. He made the most of his affluent upbringing by travelling the world in his late teenage years and throughout his twenties. First class. Unapologetic. The rumour was that he was once a roadie for Guns N' Roses, and the wall of memory in the bar studded with countless pictures confirmed that.

Every evening, office-goers and retired pros used to meet up here to call it a day. Age no bar. Just like a sitcom.

There was beer, scotch, food, music, and sports—just like a sitcom.

There was conversation and real laughter... well... unlike a sitcom.

Sharp at 6:30 PM, Amma and Ibu entered the watering hole. Both of them nodded at Balli Bhau at the counter, and the nod was accepted and returned with sincerity and a welcoming body language. Well, as welcome as Balli could be. Asif was smoking a joint at the far-right corner of the bar where the mosquito zapper was installed.

It had a name—Death Cab for Mos-Cutie. All Asif.

Amma and Ibu were greeted by the head waiter and ushered into their favourite booth like regulars. Asif quickly finished his smoke and rushed to touch their feet and take blessings. Characteristically, Asif and Balli Bhau shared many traits, but a few were starkly different too. Integrity and ethics were shared by the father-son duo, but warmth and hospitality were the differentiators. Balli Bhau was aloof and distant, but Asif was warm. He gestured to the waiter, which meant "usual." Before Amma and Ibu could settle, a huge uproar shook the entire building. There were cheers, jeers, shouts, high-fives, and chest-thumping... because Bumrah had just struck on the very first ball.

The drinks came. The duo clinked their glasses. Asif had put Dark Side of the Moon in the background at an apt volume. Amma acknowledged it and raised his glass to him. And then, for the next hour and a half, Indian bowling decimated Sri Lankan batting in a way that will go down in the books. The match ended quite early, and so did the merriment.

"Bloody dopamine... The higher the rise, the harder the fall. Now what, Ibu...?" inquired Amma.

"We go home, Amma. Let's call it a night today. Catch up on our reading, exercise for 3 days, and we play South

Africa 3 days from now. And you know what that means…" Ibu finished his glass.

As the dejected duo were walking out, Amma muttered under his breath, "Serves us right for being over-smart with all our promises to Shiksha, *yaar* Ibu. Karma!"

8

NOVEMBER 5TH, 2023

Clarence House, 8:30 PM

Shiksha had to admit to herself that Amma and Ibu were men of their word. As promised, both oldies walked 6 km every day. The 3rd and 4th of the month were dry and mundane. Today was the 5th day; India was playing South Africa, and Neel told her that it was almost an encore of the Sri Lanka match. The Indian team made a meal out of South Africa. A one-sided match gives victory but at the cost of excitement. Amma and Ibu were on their way home and would be happy and sad at the same time. Apart from the obvious happiness, the sadness would be from a well-earned night of partying, frittering away with very concentrated excitement—not what Amma had in mind. That's why Shiksha wanted to surprise them with a *mehfil*.

Neel had gone for the mixers, and Kamble Kaka was on the way. She was in total charge of the mehfil today, and Deva was a delightful helping hand. She was smiling as her inner monologue was running. She continued her chain of thought… unaware that Neel was back already and watching her.

"Amma and Ibu ate well and abstained from drinks. And Deva… well, Deva is an angel by default. Her boys deserve

45

the soirée. Drinks. Kebabs. Mutton pulao. Paneer pakoda will be there for Gau if he turns up. Well, of course, he would. He wouldn't ever leave a chance to hang out with Neel. Gau was loyal, awkward, and sweet. Mutton pulao was for Neel and Amma. It would be fun if Kamble Kaka announced we should have biryani instead. How much fun it would be to listen to Amma and Neel rant in the argument of pulao vs. biryani. How they would berate the taste buds of simple-minded biryani lovers and go on and on about the detailing of flavours pulao offers..."

"Pulao is far more intricate and superior, Ma'am..." Her chain of thought was interrupted by Neel's booming voice.

"Are you kidding me... stop it!! You're doing it again. You're following my chain of thought and flaunting it. Get out of my head, idiot," she was comically annoyed and threw a green chilli at him. Neel caught it and was grinning ear to ear.

"And by the way, it wasn't even that impressive. I know how you did that," announced Shiksha.

"Oh really... pray tell, then..." challenged Neel.

"Now, let me guess... you saw me staring at the delicately cooking mutton pulao, and all my attention was on it. I was meticulous in maintaining the flavours as the aroma was a witness to it. Also, I was smiling a lot while I chopped the coriander and took my time washing and cleaning them for later, which could only mean one thing—the classic famous pulao vs. biryani argument is playing in my head because it has already happened umpteen times, and hence your smart Alec comment..." She clapped her hands victoriously.

Visibly taken aback, Neel said, "Damn... that was impressive, Shiksha. You know deduction well now."

"Unh-Unh… I know YOU too well, Neel Mantri," said Shiksha, pulling his cheeks.

Right on cue, the crew entered. Amma, Ibu, and Gau, all hypnotised by the aroma of delicacies being cooked.

"Thank you, Shiksha… what a surprise, beta!" said Amma, patting her head.

The usual suspects were seated at the usual adda, and Gau was impatient.

"What's the matter, Gau… why do you have your panties in a bunch?" quipped Shiksha.

"Drinks are here. Kebabs are here. My paneer pakoda is here. And masala papad is here too. We are all here. Why are we not drinking…???" Gau was visibly impatient.

"Kamble is just parking. Let him come, Gau. If you must drink below the legal age, enjoy it to the fullest by clinking glasses with the law… ha ha…" Amma boomed at his own joke.

Everyone joined in. Ibu laid out the usual 6 glasses and started pouring. Shiksha banged another empty glass softly next to the dozen.

"Me too, please."

Everybody started clapping in unison at the new member.

"Another birthday, is it?" said Kamble as he entered the soirée.

"No—no, it's just that Shiksha will be joining us today." Amma picked up his glass and made sure everyone was standing in a close circle holding their drinks.

Amma continued, "Cheers to Shiksha for this beautiful soirée, and God bless you, beta."

"Hear hear," "Salud," "Shiksha, you angel."

The party was in full swing, and no one was remotely interested in stopping.

The kebabs were devoured with a vengeance, especially by Kamble. It was the third serving, and Shiksha asked Neel to order some more with just a small gesture. Neel understood and got on with business on his phone.

"Alright, Kamble, out with it now," said Amma. "Just tell us what is bothering you, and no to-ing and fro-ing, please. I demand it. Everyone refill your drinks and sit close; Kamble has something to share."

The finality with which Amma announced this left no room for negotiation. In 2 minutes, everyone was settled except Deva and Shiksha, who were in the kitchen looking over the scraps as Kamble had eaten it all.

"Early 2021, right in the middle of COVID, we caught a homicide case. A man was murdered with the back of his skull caved in from repeated blows. There were hardly any people outside, and we could not find any leads, witnesses, or even the murder weapon. So obviously, the case file is still open, and some faint regular enquiry was going on up until last week." Kamble took a pause for a gulp and a generous bite of kebab.

Seeing everyone glued to his story, he continued.

"The morning of Neel's birthday bash, I was urgently summoned by the IGP for this case. This cold, dead case whose leads are as dead as the man. He asked me to drop everything I have on my plate and personally oversee with my best team that this case is solved urgently." I was taken aback and immediately reviewed the case files to see if I had missed something. The man was from a middle-class background, nothing extraordinary, and there were no witnesses or relevant CCTVs at all. The man was not even close to the high-profile order I had just received. I saw the post-mortem report—no murder weapon on-site or nearby. He was in his 50s with a wife and 2 kids, and apparently, he was just normal. We checked his phone records—no affairs, no blackmail, basically no motive. He was rather an overtly religious and God-fearing man. There were just no clues. It's just a cold case." Kamble finished his drink and kebab serving.

"Anything out of the ordinary in the findings… Kaka… anything at all?" boomed Neel.

Everyone gave Neel an unrehearsed but almost simultaneous look, but Neel shared a quick glance with Shiksha.

"I mean, nothing relevant at all, but just as I mentioned that night about RD Burman, you know. In the interest of full disclosure… there was just this RD Burman hits CD lying next to the body, but that is hardly relevant… I mean, CD!!!! It could have no bearing whatsoever on the case, actually. It is common to find CDs in the trash these days. The picture of the CD is there with other details. I just don't know what to search for. It's a dead end. And the IGP is on my ass to expedite the closure. I mean… How?" finished Kamble while rubbing his temple.

Shiksha placed her hand on his shoulder, "Ok, Kaka… enough! You will find something, you always do. Now, c'mon everyone, last chance for last drinks because I am serving pulao in 5 minutes."

"Thank you, beta," beamed Kamble.

Everybody was busy topping off their drinks as another week of healthy habits was around the corner. The diktat had already been issued by Shiksha. Another soirée was promised 10 days from now.

"Here, Kaka, your drink!" Neel offered Kamble, who smiled and accepted.

"Thank you, Neel."

"Where is my birthday present, Kaka? You came empty-handed that day and today."

"What do you want, son?"

"The case files—just for tonight."

9

NOVEMBER 6ᵀᴴ, 2023

Clarence House, 2:00 AM

The night was darker than usual and quieter than usual. He knew what that eerie silence meant. This night was a reminder of that night. It could be a trigger, but he knew—not today. Today his thoughts were not stray for the taking. They were occupied. He remembered telling Shiksha that he could feel it coming. A puzzle. A problem to solve. The only thing that is infinitely more pleasurable than a drink and a smoke for him.

Neel took out the case files and started reading. He knew from what he had read dozens of times—never look for something. Just look. Stay away from even traces of confirmation bias. He sat there for a couple of hours reading, re-reading, and making notes. He read the whole file one more time—from front to end—and checked his notes. He had not missed anything. He got up and went to the kitchen instead of the bar. As the electric kettle was hissing the silence away, he could not wait to fix his coffee and look at his notes with fresh eyes. Neel realised his heart was racing, his hands were sweaty, and he was buzzing even before the caffeine hit.

"Is this how people feel before the first date?" He thought to himself and shrugged at the absurdity.

Here is coffee.

Here is the night.

Here are the case file notes.

Let's go.

The cocktail of caffeine and excitement made for rocket fuel in Neel. He took a deep dive into the elaborate case file, but it was his first time analysing an official document, so initial inertia was obvious. There was official language and technical terms to crack, but he was too happy and too excited, so the soldier powered through.

Neel realised that he was playing the game on somebody else's turf. There was a plethora of information—witnesses, CCTV footage, modus operandi of the crime, murder weapon, etc.—but wheat had to be separated from chaff. He crunched the key points relevant to him in a synopsis. In his language. In his format. In his style. His turf.

NAME: EKNATH PATIL

AGE: 52

HEIGHT: 5'10

ADDRESS: MAROL, ANDHERI (EAST), MUMBAI

DATE OF DEATH: JANUARY 21st, 2021, AT Around 8:00 PM.

FAMILY: WIFE - 50

SON - 22

DAUGHTER - 19

FRIENDS: SOLKAR & KHADSE. BOTH HAD NOT MET THE VICTIM FOR THE LAST THREE DAYS.

EYEWITNESSES: NONE

CCTV FOOTAGE NOTES: NONE - BLINDSPOTS/ NON-FUNCTIONING

CAUSE OF DEATH: REPEATED BLUNT FORCE TRAUMA, MAJORLY TO THE BACK OF THE SKULL

PLAUSIBLE MURDER WEAPON: THE WOUND SUGGESTS A HEAVY BAT/HAMMER WITH PROTRUSIONS AT THE BUSINESS END. IT COULD BE BARBED WIRE, METALLIC BEARINGS, OR GEMSTONES.

NOTES: SLIGHT SIGN OF STRUGGLE.

ONE SLIPPER MISSING.

R.D. BURMAN CD FOUND NEARBY.

Neel just couldn't picture a baseball bat with barbed wire around it. It seemed too reckless. Uncomfortable. Why would you carry barbed wire? It can tear clothes, bags, cause skin wounds… basically a lot of ways to leave DNA evidence. Neel didn't like it. At all.

That leaves the murder weapon as a single unit with protrusions. Gemstones?

How about that *gada* which *Bheem* used to carry? A mythological weapon which is easily available, and no-one will look for it.

Mythological weapon?

Karmic justice?

Is this revenge?

And what does the great R.D. have to do with it?

Any famous song?

Is the killer leaving a hint trapped in a song?

Neel looked up the songs on the CD to find a clue.

What is it he is not able to see?

His heart was racing fast.

Yes. Yes. Why didn't he see it before? Maybe because it is not visible.

Neel's inner monologue was fluent now.

Kaka said something. This case was ordinary. It's cold. No way the IGP is this desperate to solve this case. This case is not important. The victim is not important. Then why the urgency... And that too, now! The guy has been dead for over 2 and a half years now. It was because the killer was important.

The IGP wants to catch this killer because the killer is going to strike again. And someone knows this. Someone is spooked.

Someone influential.

Someone powerful.

Someone connected.

The most important clue here is that someone is scared, and it is very important to find that person.

But... then... R.D. Burman is equally important. He always is.

10
NOVEMBER 6TH, 2023

Mumbai, 3:30 a.m.

Life is different when you live in a 4000 sq. ft. penthouse duplex apartment on the 42nd floor of a posh building. Life is different from an apartment that towers over the city that never sleeps. Life is different when you can see the Queen's Necklace from your room and the black ocean wearing it. Life is different when there is someone at your beck and call to take care of every whim and fantasy. Food. Sex. What else?

But he knew why life is actually different here. It is because he knew the life… out there. Out there on the streets of Mumbai. The humid air reeking of struggles, broken dreams, and compromises. For 20 years, he had boarded a bus from the BMC office to Churchgate station, his face buried in the worried underarms of strangers. For 20 years, he had boarded the train at Churchgate to get down to Mira Road station. For 20 years, he had walked 3 km thereafter to reach his home and sleep on a gurgling stomach that would not be filled with one *roti* and half an onion.

"Excuse me, Sir! Sorry to interrupt you. What you ordered, Sir. Smoked duck and lobster ravioli. And your favourite—a large neat Glenfiddich. Enjoy your dinner, Sir."

Did you hear that? That's why life is different.

He mentally resolved and vowed not to let anything happen to this life. Yes, he fucked up. But it had to be done. Maybe not. But what's done is done. He remembered the day he accidentally stumbled across the murder of that guy… Eknath Patil. He knew he had seen him somewhere. He seemed fairly unimportant, but he knew he had met that person. And then it came jolting back. It was him! Murdered! Coincidence! His years and years in politics had taught him certain hard-earned lessons, and the number one was that there is no such thing as coincidence. And then he checked. There were others. Someone had been cleaning up the skeletons in his closet. He cursed himself for being this reckless. But not anymore. He couldn't allow the unknown enemy to close in anymore.

He called up the IGP and asked him to solve the case pronto. Urgently. Discreetly. Quietly. His life depended on it. He knew that. The IGP was a simple, greedy, transactional man. He was on it. He knew that, too. He couldn't eat tonight, but he finished the drink in one big gulp. And steadily, he went inside the bathroom where 2 white-blonde girls had been waiting for him for the past hour. He disrobed for the even uniform code in the bathroom and entered the shower.

He knew this life had to be protected at any cost.

11
November 6ᵀᴴ, 2023

Clarence House, 10:30 a.m.

Clarence House had almost settled into the mid-day monotony which a Mumbai Monday brings about. Shiksha was off to college. Ibu was gone to teach the slum kids. Deva was knee-deep in the kitchen and doing other chores. Amma and Neel were involved in an intense battle.

Neel put in extra effort in this attack, but Amma blunted it. His smile further infuriated Neel, who was now hell-bent on ripping the next one.

On the ground floor of Clarence House was an enormous empty space within the boundary wall, which housed 2 of the prized possessions of the residents. One was, of course, the sacrosanct sanctuary of Deva—the plants and the greens. The other was a thin strip roughly 20 yards in length and 8 feet in width, heavily flanked by nets all around. The batting rink. Amma had used his entire cricketing knowledge to make the pitch. The soil, the sand, the watering cycle, the grass, the rollers. It was a work of art, actually. And why were Amma and Neel out there? Anyone's guess is that cricket is in the air.

The pursuit of the purest title in cricket was the World Test Championship, which eluded India twice and was coveted by Indians with fervour. The Amma way to celebrate the purest form of cricket was to play it well. As a ritual, they were out there to knock a few. They were so made for each other that Amma loved to bat while Neel loved leg spin. No fights. Ever.

For some reason, both of them had their most heartfelt conversations on the pitch. Maybe it was the sportsman spirit or the love of the game, but this pitch was the venue for Amma and Neel's heart-to-heart conferences. Amma always felt it was the to and fro of the ball that drove the conversation, and most importantly, what was discussed on the pitch remained on the pitch. Strictly. No exceptions. The sportsman's code.

They were practising their warm-up routine, where Neel would stand and throw fast ones, and Amma would defend them. The leg spin with proper run-up came later. Neel threw a fast one. Amma defended. Classic forward defence.

"Are you sure, Neel, that you don't want to pursue academics at all?" Amma took a stance.

Neel had dropped out of school right before his XII board exams, citing 'absolute and utter uselessness.'

"Yes, Amma… I have decided. I don't want it. We are not made for each other." He was fidgeting with the ball and suddenly threw one, testing Amma's reflexes.

Amma knew cricket well and Neel better. Textbook defence.

"Ha Ha… When I am on the pitch, I am Sachin, my boy… Say, Neel… what will you do with your life then…?"

"Live it… I guess, Amma… I seriously want to be a private investigator because that is the only thing which keeps me… interested." Neel threw another one.

Amma blunted again and secretly wished he would have said happy instead of interested.

"Alright, Neel… let's practise your legendary leg spin now and test my defence. You know the rules. If you beat me purely, out. If I edge, of course out. If you rattle the timber… haha well, you name it. There is a silly point, short leg, first slip, and leg slip. Ok. Let's go."

There was an army of 4s and 6s placards on the adjoining wall, plastered for the ambience. There were 2 sets of red cherry test cricket balls—a dozen each netted like a bunch of oranges in a juice shop. The new ones were to swing, and the old ones were to turn and reverse swing. When the new gets old, then the old gets thrown. The circle of cricket or life, if you will.

It was important for Neel to get leg spin right. Not for him but for the man he adored—Shane Warne, who had passed away unexpectedly last year. A cruel joke.

Neel loved him. Drinks. Smokes. Drugs. Rock 'n' Roll. Women. And still, the man ruled test cricket. What a star!

Sherlock, Shahrukh, and Shane. Neel's holy trinity.

Neel picked up an old ball for the Warne tribute day but felt the shape a bit skewed. The ball had to be perfect. He picked up another one and started swirling it to intimidate Amma. Amma took the guard, smiling. Neel walked his run-up just like Warne. Had his tongue out on one side, just like Warne. Released a slow leg-spinner on the middle, raring to turn towards the first slip just like Warne. The ball just went straight, no turn—quite unlike Warne.

"Unintentional flipper… huh, Neel!" boomed Amma after blunting the delivery.

"I am not happy with the shape of the ball, Amma… let me try another one." Neel fished in the blue stocking net for another old one to turn it on.

"Alright… ready?" Neel was at the mark.

"Bring it on," retorted Amma, decisively and rhythmically striking the bat 3 times at his leg stump guard.

In came a flighted delivery, and Amma, with a long stride out, commanded a textbook defence. The short leg had no chance. Perfect defence.

"Click a picture, Neel," beamed Amma, still holding the pose.

"There is something wrong here, Amma… I still think the old balls are a little bent out of shape and skewed. It's weird because your shots don't have the power to deform them. You know what… let me try the new ones. These are useless." Neel fished for a new cherry.

"That is a very expensive tantrum, Neel Mantri… If we are throwing away slightly older balls like that, we'll pretty soon be going back to gully cricket with a hard tennis ball with a taped seam. Not that it's bad, but hey… don't discard the old beauties just like that." Amma was examining the old balls from the collection.

"Ok, Amma… ready! Let me make Warnie proud with this new ball." Neel was satisfied now. He planned a googly in his mind and tried hard to conceal his smile. Amma would play off the turn and leave if required. He would avoid the edge, for sure. And the chance of LBW was ripe.

As if everything was in slow motion, Neel walked like Warnie. Amma was ready. Neel turned his wrist upside down at the time of release ever so slightly that he was confident Amma didn't read it.

Just a slight inward deviation was what he wanted. Amma played with a straight bat and blunted the googly.

"Ha ha ha… Neel, you are so cute. Stop smiling with your eyes when you're about to deliver me a wrong 'un. Your lips were pursed, but your eyes were like a 100-watt bulb. You were up to something… hahaha," Amma threw the ball back and checked the time.

"Ok… pack up, champ. Let's eat something." Amma took off the gear and meticulously arranged it back.

"I have some work, Amma. I'll catch you later," Neel assembled all the old balls and new balls separately.

"Don't throw the old balls away, you rich spoilt brat," scowled Amma.

"Ok, Amma… point taken. But they are not just old but deformed too." Neel was sweeping the rink.

"Tell Kamble I said hello when you meet him at the police station, and best of luck, Sherlock…" Amma said on his way out, letting him know that he knew about his every move.

Neel managed to smile at the old man's smartness.

12
NOVEMBER 6TH, 2023

Andheri Police Station, Mumbai, 2:00 p.m.

Neel was waiting outside the Andheri Police Station, puffing the time away. He had texted Kamble Kaka in the morning, requesting to drop in. And he was dead sure Amma had called too after their net practice and had **put in a good word for him**. Deep in thought. Today could be the beginning of a new life for him. A life he always wanted. Solving puzzles for a living. Too good to be true. He dropped the cigarette 3-4 drags short of completion as he saw Gaurang running towards him.

"Sorry, Neel… I did the best I could…" Gau was stuttering and out of breath.

Neel asked him to bend down, place his palms on his knees, and breathe deeply, just like basketball players. Gau obeyed and felt better in a minute.

An excited Neel and a cautious Gau entered the police station, looking for Mr. Kamble. The duo was mesmerised, looking at the chaos of a police station, and were comparing the visuals with a preconceived image in their minds courtesy of movies. A curt constable ushered them into Kaka's room.

"Oye Neel… Gaurang… come, come… sit. What will you have?"

"Nothing for Neel, but I'll have a Pepsi, Kaka," quipped Gau. Kaka gestured to the attendant.

Neel leaned forward in the chair, took out the notes from the backpack, and placed them on the table. He was feeling excited to share his analysis, and he knew that Kaka could see that and had an amused look. Feeling encouraged, he began.

"Here is a synopsis of the facts I tabulated by reading the case files, Kaka." Neel handed over the reports and his notes. Kaka was genuinely interested.

Neel stood up and continued, "I have many insights here, Kaka, but I'll start with the most important and relevant one. The victim was, for the lack of a better word, ordinary or unimportant, but you were communicated that the case is extremely important."

Neel walked for 3 to 4 steps, commanding the eye-line of Kaka and Gau with him, ensuring he had their attention. Enough pause. He continued, "Two questions—Why… and Why Now?"

"Great questions," hyped Gau with a quintessential Indian head sideways bob. Kaka ignored him.

Without trying Kaka's patience, Neel softly placed both his palms on the table, leaned forward, and continued, "Because someone important is interested, and he/she just came across this case. That's why and why now." Neel waited.

"Elaborate, Neel," Kamble was still very interested.

"Kaka… the case is more than 2 and a half years old and suddenly becomes relevant! Why? Because someone has just put together a correlation between this murder and a looming danger to themselves. Why the delay? Because this ordinary person's death didn't matter until it did because… someone… made a connection." Neel was walking slowly, and Gau and Kamble were absolutely tuned in.

"And because the IGP is personally monitoring the case, it's a no-brainer that this someone is important." Neel summarised and stood still with arms crossed.

"Makes sense, Neel… Good… Now answer my questions… Why and What…" said Kamble, leaning back in his chair.

Neel and Gau shared a quizzical expression.

"Why… did you wreck your brains on this analysis… and What… do you want?" asked Kamble.

Neel sat down, put his hands on the table calmly, and softly said, "Kaka… I want to do this with my life. You know this. Let me start, please. And I am off to a good start here, aren't I? Please let me assist you with this case. I feel that I can solve this, and it is a very big case. I can feel it in my bones. Please."

Kamble was not sure what Neel actually meant or if he was even equipped enough to contribute significantly. But one thing he was sure of: he was at a dead end. There was nothing new happening; there was no new theory, no new evidence, and no new angle of investigation.

Nothing. It was a fact that the IGP was breathing down Kamble's neck, and the stress was taking its toll on him. So the question was not, Why Neel? The question was, Why not Neel? Kamble had almost reached the stage where a fresh pair of eyes couldn't hurt. But ground rules had to be established. Today's youth need to be reined in. No free hand.

"Please, Kaka…" Gau reiterated the request a little more dramatically.

"Oh, shut up, Gau… Neel, you are a sharp tool but a loose cannon. Don't give me a chance to kick your ass. This is official and serious business. Be careful. Follow orders. And don't do anything without asking and confirming with me first. Fine… you will **UNOFFICIALLY** help me on this one. Start slow and see where this takes us. Welcome aboard, Sherlock." Kamble extended his hand.

Neel grabbed it with both hands and chuckled, "Oh, thank you, Kaka… I have more to share, but give me some time to formulate my thoughts. Can I see you tomorrow again at the same time? I mean, can you give me 15 minutes to report my findings every day, please?"

"Fine. And slow down, Neel." Kaka signed off.

The boys came out of the police station and found some shade to catch their breath. Neel was smiling, and Gau was high-fiving and hollering. No hugs, though. He knew.

"How do we… I mean… you start?" came the question from Gau.

"We start with lunch followed by some legwork, my dear Gau."

"Legwork… good, good. You know what they say. Never miss leg days in the gym."

Neel was already gone.

13

NOVEMBER 6TH, 2023

5:00 p.m., Patil Residence

Amidst the unpredictable, ever-looming Mumbai rains, Neel was out with Gau for the "legwork." The legendary Sherlock Holmes admitted that his elder brother Mycroft was an even match for his extraordinary mental abilities but could never be as good a detective. The reason was the absence of energetic and tireless pursuit of truth. The legwork.

Neel rang the bell, and looking at the clean foyer outside, he knew someone was definitely in. The door opened, and a sombre-looking middle-aged woman stared at them with a quizzical expression.

"Hello, Ma'am… sorry to disturb you. I am Neel, and this is Gaurang. We are consulting detectives working with Kaka… err… I mean Senior Police Detective Rachit Kamble. Are you Mrs. Patil, Ma'am?"

The lady stiffened up and scanned both the boys sternly.

Her body language was understandably unwelcome, and her guardedness was augmented further as she was not convinced that these 2 boys were consulting detectives. There was silence and mistrust in the air for a minute. Her fight-or-flight response was triggered.

Neel picked up on that, took a step back, and gestured for Gau to do the same.

He softened his stance and tone.

"Ma'am… Actually, Kamble sahib is our uncle, and he is the chief investigating officer in the death… I mean the case of Mr. Eknath Patil. Sorry to come unannounced like this, but we are assisting Kaka in the case, and we would love it if you could give us just 15 minutes of your time, please?" Gau was amazed at this empathetic Neel but kept his soft gaze towards the still-hostile lady.

Neel took out his notes and went through the questions he had in mind. Gau was just looking around, seated on the single sofa facing the balcony, thinking about how he could be of importance. And then the phone rang.

"Neel… *chutiye*… what the fuck are you doing there? I let you in a minute ago, pointing out that you are a loose cannon… and you are at the victim's house. How dare you…? Without telling me?… She is not angry, but she wants you to leave right now. Just leave… right now, and the next time I see you, I am going to carve out the Swiss national flag on your ass. Leave… noooowwww!!!"

He was not afraid of Kaka the softie. He was disappointed. He didn't come across as earnest enough to the lady for her help. That was a major downer in the future career he was eyeing.

Neel started receding and gestured to Gau to leave, and right at the end of the foyer, he turned around and could see the lady still looking through a sliver.

"Ma'am, it's painful to lose someone, and believe me, I know. You can't change that, and I can't change that, but not knowing who did this is even more painful, and believe me, I know that even better. I have lost my mother, and I don't know why, and I don't know who to blame. He is still out there, and that kills me every day. I am not here to carelessly fiddle with your trauma but to render a fresh perspective on the case. I want to solve this for you. For closure, so to speak. But I am sorry if we crossed the line. Good day, ma'am."

As Neel and Gau trod out, a voice boomed *"Chai peeyoge…?"*

Fifteen minutes of silence and anticipation later, Mrs. Patil was sitting in front of the sleuths in her living room for a conversation. Her body language was now neutral, and she was almost blank in her expressions, but Neel could sense that she wanted this Q&A because of the most powerful drug in the world—hope.

"Anything you can tell me, Ma'am, about your husband that stands out, as I am sure you have racked hours of thinking to find anything unusual which might be a lead…" And then Neel leaned back to suggest that it was her turn to speak, and he was all ears.

Mrs. Patil, after 2 sips of the chai, stared into nothing and began talking.

"He was a good man, a simple man, an ordinary man but a great husband and father. We met in college during our sophomore year. He was transferred from a college in a remote village in Maharashtra in his second year owing to his academic brilliance. I saw him as a gawky teen just petrified of this city and the steely resolve in his eyes of never surrendering. I loved the simplicity… so refreshing." She went quiet. Gau quizzically looked at Neel, but no one interrupted. Suddenly, she burst out laughing and said, "You know how he proposed… he said… ummm… Pragya, can you please marry me? I would be highly obliged." Her chuckle continued and gave way to a stifled sob in an instant.

She recovered and continued, "Eknath and I were happy and, most importantly, content. We always had more than enough. The kids were on the right track, and we could afford their education, as I said. I mean… he worked for the state government… so there was no stress of losing his job as well… I mean… so religious… so God-fearing… I mean… I just don't understand…"

Neel waited patiently and asked the redundant but important question.

"Do you think anyone would have wanted to harm your husband, Ma'am?"

"No. Absolutely not," said Mrs. Patil firmly.

"Ok, Ma'am. Here is a request. Without ever taking your time for granted, can we come back if we have more questions, please? We just want to help, and we will call and get permission first."

November 6th, 2023
Juhu Beach, 7:00 p.m.

Say what you want, but sunset at Juhu Beach accompanied with butter-laden pav bhaji can turn around anyone's day. Neel and Gau landed at the beach for the same gastronomic gaiety.

As Gau was ordering, Neel took out his phone to record an audio message.

"Kamble Kaka… I am very sorry for today. I have tried to make things right with the lady, but I promise I will not overextend my welcome with you like this again. First and last mistake. Apologies. Please forgive me."

He sent it to Kaka and made a mental note of being more professional and avoiding fuck-ups like that. He was a little disappointed in himself, to say the least.

Sunset. Ocean. Lovely breeze. Pav bhaji with loads of butter. But Neel was lost. Grim. Gau was busy inhaling while Neel's plate was untouched. Reluctantly, Gau had to stop eating.

"You are so hard on yourself, Neel; you don't need the world to judge you. Oh, c'mon… it was an honest mistake, emanating out of over-enthusiasm and over-excitement. You are a starter sleuth. Learn on the job, man."

That was all he managed because Gau couldn't wait to put another morsel in his mouth. Neel was just staring at the horizon. No eye contact. Finally, he spoke.

"Gau, I rate myself very high, you know, and I don't expect myself to be this reckless. I can't be making mistakes like… well, normal people. Now, what if Kaka holds me back on this case from now on? He could keep me around but could not trust me anymore, you know. I have decided not to pursue academics at all, not because I am a hippie only in the soul Gau, not in the way I live or I want to live. I like finer things in life, and they cost money. I love money, and I love what money can do or what one can do with money. This is not a hobby. This is not a college project. This is it. Being a detective is what I want to do. Criminal consultancy is what I covet. I can't be reckless. That's not me." He was still staring at the horizon, but Neel was breathing heavily. Gau realised the gravity of the situation.

"Okay, okay, I get it. First and last mistake. That's it."

Ding came the sound of a notification. "It's yours," said Gau, licking his fingers.

It was a message from Kaka.

"You are forgiven, chutiya. That lady called me again. She requested your unofficial association with me. I don't know what you said, but you are ON!!!"

Neel smiled and looked at Gau and didn't have to say anything.

"See… I told you. Now, c'mon, give me half of your Pav Bhaji." It was not a request.

14.
November 6ᵀᴴ, 2023

Clarence House, 10:30 PM

Dinner was done in Clarence House. All the oldies had retired to their respective rooms, and a welcome quiet had spread around. Neel liked it. He was standing at the edge of the terrace and staring at the moon while smoking the quintessential after-dinner cigarette. Smiling.

"Now, now… what has happened to you today?" Neel was startled.

"What do you mean… happened… today…" inquired Neel and let out an audible exhale.

"You ate palak-daal without fuss, you had one roti more than usual… and you are almost smiling since you got here. What has happened?" Shiksha parked herself on the chair and stretched her legs on the table.

Neel carefully stubbed the cigarette on the sole of his shoe and kept the stump in his hand to be thrown away later.

"Today marks the beginning of Shiksha. This is it. I am no longer directionless. I really want to become a detective, and I just took the first step. You know I want to share everything with you, but not just today. I am too excited. I want to work. I need to work. Good night."

Neel kissed her forehead, rushed to his room, and shut the door.

"Of course, I understand, Neel…" Shiksha sighed.

NOVEMBER 7ᵀᴴ, 2023
Clarence House, 1:00 AM

He had been wrecking his brain with the available information for over 2 hours now. It was time. Neel truly believed that half the problem would be solved if you could write it down exactly. The nerd inside Neel wanted to do just that. He took out his long book and fished his pen out. A beautiful fountain pen. He opened a middle page wide. On the left page was "THINGS I KNOW," and on the right, "THINGS I SHOULD KNOW/ASK." Here goes:

<u>THINGS I KNOW</u>

- The victim died of blunt force trauma inflicted by a heavy bat with some protrusions at the business end.
- There is nothing extraordinary about the victim and his family which suggests a possible culprit or motive.
- The case was unsolved but cold until it was revived by the IGP, and an ultimatum was given to Kaka.
- Someone has already solved the case, at least the motive of the murder, not the murderer. Someone powerful who can influence the IGP. Someone big and, more importantly, someone scared for his/her own life. (maybe?)

<u>THINGS I SHOULD KNOW/ASK</u>

- What are the possible murder weapons or contraptions that can fit the bill? The idea of a mythological weapon like **BHEEM ki GADA** cannot be brushed aside.
- The victim had something to hide for sure. It's not obvious. It's not visible. His family doesn't know (maybe?). There is a skeleton in the closet to be discovered.
- Who is someone? Who is influencing the IGP? Is he/she next? Is this vendetta/personal? Investigate the IGP.
- And of course… R.D. Burman CD.

Neel took a picture and sent it to The 3 Musketeers and Kaka. For a minute, he was tempted to add Kaka to the group but decided against it. Now, it was time for some sleep. He had to sleep as it was going to get busier every day now. He hated it, but he loved what he was doing more.

15

April 4ᵗʰ, 2011

"*Oye, goongey... idhar aa,*" The scrawny kid was summoned by the gang of bullies. He had no choice but to obey.

"We have heard you deliberately don't talk because of some trauma bullshit," said the bigger alpha. The kid just kept quiet and kept looking. Straight at him. Or maybe through him.

"You know what I think? I think he stammers really bad, so bad that keeping quiet is a better option," said one of them, and they all laughed in unison. The kid kept staring back.

"What are you looking at, asshole… huh… look down." He didn't.

"Look down," the alpha slapped him. He still didn't.

They pushed him on the ground and started kicking and abusing him. He didn't speak. He didn't cry. He didn't beg. He didn't fight back. He just didn't.

"*Oyeee,* assholes," a voice boomed. Bang came the cricket bat on the head of the lead alpha, and he collapsed on the ground. This all happened in a flash. The rest of them were just shocked and staring at the saviour. Saviour with a cricket bat.

"You want one… hook shot. Just like him." He was pointing at the lead alpha, who was still writhing in pain, holding his head. The saviour was red with anger. Anybody could tell he meant business. Just a kid, but he would beat all of them up for sure.

They all retreated and chose to back off. Obviously.

"And listen…," they all stopped, "if you hurt him next time, I promise you I will strike your head for a 6. Try me." He swung his bat on his shoulders as he finished his warning.

"You are Neel Mantri, right?" the saviour inquired, and the kid nodded.

"I am Gaurang. We are in the same class." They shook hands as Neel nodded in agreement.

"Oh, you know me. I thought we had never spoken… I mean, you have not spoken… I mean… leave it. By the way, you can call me Gau… I mean, if you want." Gau gripped the bat like a batsman and took the stance.

"We are world champions, Neel. We won the World Cup the day before yesterday. Dhoni hit a 6 to seal the deal, you know." Gau mimicked the same shot and held his pose for effect. For almost too long and continued.

"This is new INDIA. We will not be bullied. We just won't."

Neel smiled as if he was amused with this boy, Gau. But it was the beginning of a new friendship. They both knew.

16
November 7th, 2023

Mumbai, 1:15 PM

Most men are creatures of habit. They don't like to change much. Probably because they are simple beings who prefer routines. Even the well-dressed, well-spoken, metrosexual guys like Gaurang Bedi, with their whims and idiosyncrasies, love a routine. Gau liked his lazy lunch after college lectures. Then, a big glass of buttermilk. But not today. He burst out of the lecture hall, grabbed a vada-pav on the go from the college canteen, hailed a rickshaw, parked himself without confirmation and huffed, "Andheri Police Station, please."

The reason is Neel. Neel needs him. And he will be on time. Not even 5 minutes' delay. He was excited and happy for Neel. Finally, he found, thanks to repetitive social media content, his ***ikigai***.

Gaurang found himself at the Andheri Police Station main gate at 1:29 PM, with Neel standing right on the sidewalk smoking a quick one. He paid the fare and stood right in front of Neel, "1:30 PM, Neel."

"Thanks, Gau…" said Neel, stubbing the cigarette. "Let's go."

Honestly, Gau was a bit hurt at the zero celebrations over the man's punctuality.

Neel entered the room, holding his ears with both his hands. This was the most popular Indian gesture for when a kid is seriously sorry. He went up to Kaka and squatted down in front of him, maintaining the hand position and completing the apology. Kaka smiled and gently slapped him. "Go sit there. It's okay. Never again. Nautanki."

Kaka took out the list of things Neel had messaged the previous night.

"Let me take us through them one by one, Kaka," Neel offered before Kaka could say anything, and by the look of it, he wanted it this way. Neel sat ramrod straight in his chair and began.

"The murder weapon is intriguing, Kaka; we have to consider all the possibilities. The 2 factors in my mind are either the weapon is making or being shown to make a statement by someone, or it is hiding in plain sight." Kaka was listening intently, and Gau was nodding with an intense look of approval in support.

"Secondly, I refuse to believe that Mr. Patil lost his life coincidentally. It was not a mugging. It was in the middle of peak COVID. The blind spots of CCTV cameras suggest prior reconnaissance of the murder site and the victim's routine. So either the family knows... something... something worth killing for... and is still hiding it because it may have consequences for the survivors or..." Neel deliberately paused for effect to check the attention level of the audience.

"...Or...?" Both Gau and Kaka uttered in perfect unison. Neel was feeling it.

"…or they don't know that they know something. I mean, something is there which the family may not have thought important enough to be mentioned, but it is… wildly important," finished Neel with poise as he leaned back, letting them—especially Kaka—stew in his observations.

The room was silent. Neel was looking at Kaka. Kaka was deep in thought. Gau was rocking his gaze back and forth between them, waiting for someone to say something. Finally, Kaka spoke.

"Both observations make sense, Neel, but are far too intangible to achieve anything concrete. So I guess…" he raised both his hands as if what Neel was about to say was the obvious starting point.

"Yes, Kaka. I agree. Our first order of business should be to figure out the influential person behind the IGP's orders. He/she is either a billionaire businessman, a very successful politician, or both. We find him/her, and we are inside the door." Kaka nodded in agreement.

Silence again. The 2 of them deep in thought.

Finally, it was Gau's turn. "We can track the past career graph of the IGP. I'm sure he has been bouncing from place to place. Any influential common name which appears way too many times to be a coincidence, BAM, that's our guy… or girl, you know…" finished Gau in one breath.

Neel and Kaka were smiling ear to ear. Gau was making sense. Neel was proud.

"Okay… so, Kaka. Please see if you can find our influential person by tracking the IGP's history. Meanwhile, I will meet the family, especially Mrs. Patil, one more time to see if I missed something…"

"Absolutely not. You are careless…" roared Kaka.

"Kaka… Kaka… I will be sensitive, and most importantly, I will ask permission to meet. I promise, Kaka. I intend on doing this for life. I will not mess this up," said Neel earnestly with folded hands.

"Please, Kaka…" Gau joined in.

"Shut up, Gau," Kaka was successful in hiding his smile.

Neel whipped out his phone and was typing a meeting request to Mrs. Patil, an honest message laden with politeness and decency. Meanwhile, Gau mustered the courage and asked.

"Ummm, Kaka… can I…" A pause.

"Can I… what…?" The pause was spliced in 2.

"I mean… Neel and I were wondering if we can add you to our group. There are just 3 of us, including Shiksha. I mean, now it would be 4… if you say…" Gau elbowed Neel.

Neel was done. He showed the message to Kaka. "There, Kaka, if she says yes, I will call or meet her only then. Everything by the book from here on." Neel stood up and was about to leave when he turned around abruptly.

"The Four of Us, and for short F4… is that name okay for the new group, Kaka…?"

Kaka gave a thumbs up and dove into the file.

Gau, visibly offended, muttered under his breath, "How dry and uncreative! I had something else in mind—The Fabulous Foursome…"

Neel was already out of the room, and Kaka was too tired to say, "Shut up, Gau."

17
November 7ᵀᴴ, 2023

Mumbai, 2:30 PM

Neel & Gau

Much to Gau's chagrin, there were 3 thumbs-up emoticons in the brand-new group F4. Not to seem snooty, Gau became the fourth responder, and the official communication channel had been established. Though Shiksha had no idea what was happening, she was confident Neel would get her up to speed at night.

The boys were headed in a rickshaw to Mrs. Patil's house. She had promptly replied to Neel's request and agreed to meet them in an hour. Neel was genuinely pleased with the connection he was able to establish with her after a turbulent start. He made a mental note to flaunt this display of empathy and soft skills in front of Shiksha tonight.

Kaka

Meanwhile, in the police canteen, Kaka was indulging in some office politics. He identified the most gossip-loving group of policemen and casually sat at their table with his dabba. Kamble had a reputation for being an honest cop, which, translated into the cop-verse, meant inflexible and uncompromising. Problematic, basically. So Kamble had to break the ice first.

"Kya, Kamble, what are you doing here in our neck of the woods?" inquired Shinde, the king of gossipmongers.

"Had to decompress my head, Shinde Bhau, our IGP Mr. Deven Gadhvi is driving me nuts." Kamble was careful not to overact. Natural acting was required here, and Kamble was successful so far.

If there's one thing misery loves, it's company. Love could be a gentle unifier, but hate wins hands down. Two people hating on and complaining about the same guy can be instant best friends. Shinde was triggered at the right place and maybe at the right time.

"Arey, fuck him… he is just one giant bootlicker who has brown-nosed his way to the top. *Do kawdi ki aukaat nahi thi haraami ki, but… kismet re, Kamble… naseeb hai…"* Shinde was almost dejected when he was done talking.

"But how… whose ass does he kiss, *yaar…*?" Kamble banged his spoon on the plate in the middle of a performance of a lifetime.

Shinde stopped eating, leaned closer, and said, "Mantralaya… the whole consortium of ministers. Gadhvi has been going to the Ministers Block almost every Tuesday for the last 2 months. Why…? Think…?"

"But there has to be one special… his Godfather…" Kamble spoke, still chewing.

"That… I don't know, *baba…"* Shinde suddenly clammed up. Cop instincts. A cop is never comfortable divulging information. As far as intel goes, it's incoming only. Kamble sensed that Shinde was feeling exposed, so it was time for some clichés to control the damage.

"Sahi hai, Shinde… our time will also come. Maybe someday we will also drive a BMW." Kamble sounded genuinely despondent. He was even surprised by his flawless delivery. Shinde took the bait.

"Not just a BMW, Kamble, even a flat in Worli worth 15 crores… all paid up." Shinde winked and continued. "To know about a celebrity in question, one can be a better resource than his driver or… PA…" Shinde winked, finished his last morsel of **daal**, and left the table.

"And… your luck, Kamble… today is Tuesday, by the way…" Shinde gave a parting gift.

Neel & Gau

"This chai is just… magic!" exclaimed Gau after a loud and generous typically Indian slurp and was met with a curt expression from Neel and a rare smile from Mrs. Patil.

"This was Eknath's favourite. Adrak chai and pakoda. Simple man. Simple pleasures. Simple life." She took another sip from the tea, and silence was in the air again, begging to be broken.

"Anyway… ask me what you wanted to ask…" Mrs. Patil was in the moment again.

Neel fished out his notebook and pen. "Ma'am, I am going to jog your memory with some brisk questions. Please try to answer without thinking much… I mean, let your gut be the guide… Please… this is important." Neel was ready and alert. Mrs. Patil nodded gently in agreement.

"Was your husband stressed or depressed lately? And please think back from now to 3 to 4 years ago…" Neel started the questionnaire.

"No, not at all. The usual. However, the stress was obviously there during the peak delta wave of COVID-19 for the safety of our family. Our daughter, Vaishali, caught COVID twice and was very serious during those dreadful times."

Neel was quite happy with the perfect detailing of the answer. It was important to set the baseline for details. This would come in handy with the questions that followed. He gave the notepad and pen to Gau and gestured for him to take notes. He just wanted to focus on the line of questioning now.

"Are you rich… I mean… was your husband rich?"

Mrs. Patil didn't mind the directness.

"No. But as I said before, we were comfortable. Quite comfortable," she concluded.

"Okay… was he religious… I mean rituals… fasting… you know…"

"Yes, he was. He was compassionate, God-fearing, and religious. Quite the ideal husband. He was happy. We were happy." There was a sense of finality in her statement, which disappointed Neel. He decided to go for it.

"Okay, Ma'am… you knew him for 25 years… so let me ask you this…" He leaned forward, and so did Gau. "…Was he *always* religious… *always* comfortable… financially, I mean?"

The stress of the word "always" was still echoing in the room, and Mrs. Patil understood the assignment because she was thinking intently. Neel leaned back in wait, and Gau did too.

Mrs. Patil checked and formulated something in her head and looked at Neel again.

"No… no, he wasn't always these things."

Bingo. Neel was alert now. More than usual.

"He was always working before. The kids were little. His salary was inadequate, so he kept moonlighting for small assignments as a freelancer. So, no God, no family… all work it was initially. But once he came into some money due to inheritance from his ancestral land in the village, he became so relieved and thankful that he changed…" Mrs. Patil was thinking again.

Neel took advantage of the pause.

"Can you say that… he almost changed overnight…?"

She met his gaze and understood something.

"Yes… we can say that. He almost changed overnight…" She let it hang there and got lost in thoughts again.

Gau was about to say something, but Neel gestured for him to be quiet. He knew the mental mathematics she was doing, and nothing good could come out of interrupting her now.

"It all started around New Year's, as if our prayers were answered. The sudden inheritance came, and he was relieved. More at home. Instead of living it up, he gave up alcohol, paan masala, cigarettes, and even non-veg food. Even prawns—his favourite. He said that was his way of offering his heartfelt thanks to God for these sudden blessings."

She was sobbing again. Neel waited patiently, and Gau found a napkin holder on the side table and offered it to her. She fished one out and appreciated the gesture.

"It all made sense… it was New Year's… newfound money… newfound happiness… and, most importantly… gratitude. He changed for the better. I mean… you get it, right?" sniffled Mrs. Patil.

"Yes, Ma'am, I understand. Just a couple of things…"

She looked at Neel expectantly.

"Is there a way you can try and trace this inheritance money your husband received? And the second thing… may I ask when did this transformation happen?"

"This was around… New Year's… January 2011… and I will try to call up and confirm about the money…"

Neel got up. "Thank you, Ma'am. This was very helpful. As promised before, I will be in touch, and I promise you I will solve this. My request is, please talk to your kids. If you or they recall anything relevant or out of the ordinary, then please call me. Please. … Let's go, Gau."

"Thank you for the magical chai, Aunty," grinned Gau.

"Neel…" The voice made them stop and turn around.

"Do you think he was involved in something shady… I mean, was he guilty… of… something…?"

"I don't know, Ma'am, but I have a feeling he was a victim… of… something."

KAKA

Kamble saw firsthand proof of 2 old adages in the political circles of Mumbai. One is ***chai se zyada ketli garam***, and the other is ***Mantri se zyada powerful Mantri ka PA hota hai.*** Prakash Patil, aka PP, the Personal Assistant to IGP Deven Gadhvi, and Paul, the driver to IGP, were standing beneath a tree smoking what looked like imported cigarettes. Their aura reeked of power, money, and superiority. One glance, and Kamble could tell that these 2 were living way beyond their means because of, well, IGP saheb. But there is no free lunch. They must be handsomely paid to be complicit in unsavoury things sometimes and speak only when spoken to. In fact, money is paid most of the time to actually not say anything and look the other way.

"Hey PP... hey Paul... what is happening?" Kamble asked sheepishly.

"Kya, Kamble..." said PP while Paul just nodded and almost puffed in Kamble's face.

A driver and a PA had the audacity to speak so coldly and indifferently to a senior police detective. Kamble was furious but knew it was not them. It was the power. He had a renewed desire to deflate these assholes someday, so he swallowed his pride and continued.

"I must admit, guys... I envy your lifestyle. And also, your dressing sense and even the cigarette brand you smoke. What style, guys!" Vanity, thy name is man, Kamble hoped.

"Arey, Kamble, we will get you a full carton tonight itself. That custom shop is right next to Mantralaya. Boss has a meeting today at 5:00. Don't worry." Paul could have gone on, but PP nudged him quiet. Kamble sensed Paul was the loose cannon, but PP was careful.

"Thank you, yaar Paul, and also for your watch, PP. What swag, bhau..."

"Arey, this was a gift from Chavan Saheb's driver..." Paul was interrupted by PP. He gestured for him to be quiet, and in a flurry, they stubbed out their cigarettes and rushed to the car parked right at the entrance.

IGP Gadhvi was out, heading towards the car. A flurry of salutes went around, and the man was whisked away in his BMW with a red cherry on top, maybe to Mantralaya. Maybe to meet some Chavan. Kamble flipped out his phone, and a quick search turned his smile upside down into a frown. There were 5 Chavans in the Mantralaya.

Anyway, it was a start. Maybe the lads had a breakthrough, he hoped.

18
November 7TH, 2023

Mumbai, 5:30 PM

His residence was a 4,000 sq. ft. penthouse duplex on the 42nd floor because his office was on the 4th floor of Mantralaya. Power begets power. Tall buildings are built on foundations, but castles are built on graveyards sometimes. He knew that his journey had been on a steep rise so far purely because of his ruthlessness. There is no scope for error. That is why he was mad at himself. How could he be careless enough not to monitor the problem until it was entirely gone? Anyway… damage control time. Sub-Inspector Gadhvi was waiting outside the door for further instructions. IGP Gadhvi would always remain a Sub-Inspector for him. He was the same rat that he was 12 years ago. Eight promotions in 12 years, Gadhvi better deliver.

He also knew that Special Detective Kamble was on the case. But this threat that had posed itself needed to be neutralised. Pronto, and Gadhvi/Kamble were butter knives— not the sharpest. He had to help… more. Even though it was a risk, he had to take it. The murder of Eknath Patil needed to be solved pronto, and that murderer needed to be murdered pronto. It was a calculated risk. Besides,

Kamble was not sharp enough to trace all the way back to the day, and even if he caught a whiff, the case would be closed by then, and he would be transferred. He settled beside the corner window of the office, looking outside at the city. He wanted to rule completely, but he was still a step short of the throne. Very soon. Bloody soon. And nothing can stop him. It was time to call that rat, Gadhvi.

"Send that idiot in," his voice boomed.

The door opened, and Gadhvi entered with a file and a grin. "Namaste, Chavan Saheb!"

He did not turn around, was still staring outside the window, and had not even offered a seat yet. Gadhvi was sharp enough to gauge the mood and kept standing.

"Does Kamble know that you... I am... driving this?"

"No, Saheb. I haven't..." Gadhvi was blatantly interrupted.

"Practice minimalism, Gadhvi. Monosyllabic answers are the best. Elaborate only when required. Pick up that red file on my desk. It has been a cold case since January 2019. Give this to Kamble. This should help."

He turned around and steadily walked to his chair, seating himself in an assured manner. Gadhvi was still standing and was waiting for permission to speak. He was now making eye contact and nodded his head and eyebrows in anticipation.

"Saheb... what if it leads to... the day..." Gadhvi was glad he was blatantly interrupted again.

"No, it won't... you won't let it happen, Gadhvi. Right? Your life depends on it. Doesn't it? Take daily updates from Kamble. Be a step ahead of him. We don't need proof, Gadhvi. All we need is a suspect list. We will eliminate all of them if required. Do you know what will happen if the past comes out, Gadhvi?" He lit a cigarette.

Gadhvi was smart enough to understand the answer to this rhetorical question.

"It will eat you alive. Now, you don't want that... do you?"

The question was rhetorical again, but Gadhvi found himself shaking his head in a "no."

"Take the file and hand it over to Kamble. Be on top of things, and I hope that you have a suspect list for me by next Tuesday. I need this matter to be closed in a week, Gadhvi..." He puffed out a thick one.

"Ji, Saheb..." Gadhvi took the file, gave an overcompensating salute, and left with whatever dignity he thought he had left.

KAKA

A quick search revealed all possible options for Kamble. It was time to put an update on the F4 group. Kamble wanted to be the first one to post an update to set the standard tone. Crisp. To the point. Relevant information only. And above all... most importantly... complete words and punctuation if and when required. He drafted the update and pressed send. It read:

Our person of interest is a minister in the current government with the last name Chavan. The possible options are:

- *Srikant Chavan (Power)*
- *Pradeep S. Chavan (Urban Planning)*
- *Kaustubh Chavan (Public Works)*
- *Ramesh Chavan (Home & Interior Security)*
- *Satish J. Chavan (Textile)*
  Hopefully, I will get a confirmation by EOD.

NEEL & GAU

The boys were on their way to meet Shiksha in a semi-popular watering hole in the outskirts of Juhu. The place was called Paul's. It had a lazy energy, just like its name. Although the legal age to drink in a bar was technically 25, Paul's didn't make a fuss about it if one was at least 21. It was a matter of principle to Paul: if you can vote or marry, you can definitely drink. They reached and occupied a corner booth. Shiksha was running 5 minutes late. Neel asked Gau to fetch drinks while he posted the updates, as Kaka had beaten them to it. He drafted the post, which read:

> ***"Our victim, Eknath Patil, came into sudden money. He suddenly became religious. He suddenly became compassionate. The transformation was overnight, and the reason cited was gratitude for the sudden inheritance which had changed their lives. Mrs. Patil is going to confirm the money's origins. All of this happened in January 2011 around New Year's."***

Neel proofread the message one more time and hit send. Gau was back with 3 chilled beers, and Shiksha slid into the booth with them to do the honours. The trio clanked the glasses, and each had a big gulp, showing the group the kind of day they had. Shiksha and Gau were halfway through while Neel finished the pint and softly placed the empty bottle in the corner. He wasn't proud of it. He let out a loud burp that he was proud of. Gau and Shiksha burst out laughing, and Neel asked the waiter for another one.

"I read both the updates, guys. It looks like a double breakthrough, huh?" inquired Shiksha.

"Yes, definitely. I have a feeling that we have found the right thread… in fact, multiple threads actually, and if we give the right pull…" Neel was deep in thought.

"What is on your mind, Neel? This is progress… right?" Shiksha was trying to cheer him up. The waiter was back with another beer. Neel grabbed the bottle, took a big swig, still looking in a trance as if formulating his next sentence.

"Yes, yes… definitely. It's the next step… but…" he took a swig mid-sentence.

"But… what???" Gau was growing impatient.

Neel put down the bottle.

"See, the 2 most important things which lead us to a suspect are Motive and Modus Operandi, aka the murder weapon, and we have none. So maybe this is progress, or maybe it is just an isolated snippet which could lead nowhere…" Neel shrugged his shoulders as he was speaking.

"Here is an isolated snippet which could lead somewhere… check out that guy in the purple shirt. He is totally checking you out, Shiksha. Damn, he is cute too…" Gau stopped talking and took a sip.

Both Neel and Shiksha turned their attention to the distant admirer. What Gau said was true. The guy waved and Shiksha smiled and waved back.

"What are you doing, Shiksha?" Neel was alert now.

"What…!! He is cute and sweet, so I am reciprocating the gesture. That's all," toyed Shiksha.

"Well, well, well… is Neel Mantri jealous?" Gau was visibly and audibly amused. Shiksha was smiling and waiting for the answer.

"Oh come on… I was just saying… that… I mean… we are in the middle of something here… I mean… let's focus, guys…" simpered Neel.

Gau and Shiksha could not resist a high 5 as Neel's face showed all kinds of red. Suddenly Neel's phone rang. It was Mrs. Patil. Neel rushed out to attend the call.

"Saved by the bell…" Both Gau and Shiksha shot a parting comment in unison, still snickering.

Neel was out now. He pressed the green button and blurted almost immediately, "Yes, Ma'am… tell me…"

"Uhhh… you were right… The money trail did not hold. There are no relatives, no ancestral property, no inheritance… Eknath lied to me… He is gone, and he lied to me…" she started sobbing.

"Ma'am… could you please have some water… and please take your time… can I call you back in some time if that is okay?"

"No, no… I am fine now… tell me…" Mrs. Patil regained her composure.

"Ma'am, just one question… who did your husband say he inherited from? I mean, I know there is no one like that in the village, but what was the name?"

"He didn't give a full name… he just said that they used to call him… RC Kaka."

Kaka

Kamble was waiting. IGP Gadhvi had not returned yet. However, there was a high chance he was not coming. He was in South Bombay for the meeting. His house was in Worli. He wouldn't come all the way to Andheri in the evening just to drive halfway back again. He didn't need to. He was the boss. But Kamble never assumed anything. That was his strength. Also, he was excited now. He felt a renewed vigour to solve this. It was driven by the detective inside him and the desire to put the Gadhvis and Chavans of the world in their place. He could feel the excitement as he saw the BMW with the red cherry roll in, and as he peeped in, he understood the lesson—be careful what you wish for. Only Paul, the driver, and PP, the personal assistant, were there. Kamble started walking towards his bike as PP called out his name. He stiffened and was angry again about the disrespect on that call.

"Oye Kamble… Gadhvi Saheb has asked you to be in the office at 10:00 AM sharp tomorrow. Don't be late. Ok." PP lit one.

Kamble knew he had to act his ass off. These 2 were assholes, but they were useful assholes.

"Ok, PP Saheb… but get me also a watch like that, na… Ask Chavan Saheb's driver for one more, no please…." Kamble was dripping with fake honey. PP smiled but was unmoved.

"Arey, when Ramesh Chavan Saheb becomes the Chief Minister naa… the driver promised me 2 new watches, Kamble. I will give one to you…" PP pushed Paul before he could finish, but the cat was out of the bag. Kamble was smiling ear to ear.

"Thank you, Paul Bhau… ok, PP. Good Night." As PP was scolding Paul, Kamble started his bike and rolled out of the police station. As soon as he was out of sight, he fished out his mobile and fired the F4 group open. The message from Neel said:

"Kaka, it's RC. Ramesh Chavan."

Kaka smiled and typed away:

"Yes, it's Ramesh Chavan for sure. Urgent meeting with Gadhvi at 10 in the morning. Don't come to the police

station now. Let's meet outside. Call me when you reach the station tomorrow. And listen… my gut tells me it's going to be messy and exhausting. We need rest and all the help we can find."

NEEL & SHIKSHA

Gau had gone back home. He had to copy some assignment, and the last date of submission was yesterday. It was 10:30 PM. Amma and Ibu maintained discipline on the days when India was not playing. Deva too had retired. Neel sat down and immediately fired his computer on.

"*Arey*, no drinks and joint today… Neel Mantri…???"

"No… I need some help to distract me, Shiksha. This case is enough dope right now. Besides, I have some reading to catch up on… so…"

"Neel Mantri is a good boy…" Shiksha pulled both his cheeks. "Good Night."

As she was about to climb down the stairs, Neel interrupted… "Shiksha… you were right."

"Right about what…?"

"I was jealous back there in the bar. Good Night."

19
NOVEMBER 8ᵀᴴ, 2023

Mumbai, 7:30 AM

KAKA

Now that the kids were off to school, Rashmi Kamble could breathe normally. She was an English Literature major taking care of her 2 kids full time. Though she could argue vehemently in favour of a housewife being a full-time job, she found the whole thing a bit of a cliché. But it did sting, though. Her kids were grown enough now not to need her that much. They were suddenly aware of their personal space and freedom. So, Rashmi Kamble was now a perpetually angry woman. But she had to give credit to Rachit; he didn't impose anything on her. That is the beauty of Indian society. Women at large continue to do what they have been doing all this while; it's just that nowadays, they are made to believe that it was their decision. Why blame corporate culture? It just mimics life!

Lost in thoughts, she made 2 cups of tea, almost like muscle memory. It was almost 8:00 AM now, and she remembered Rachit asking her not to let him sleep late. He was looking tense. More than usual. He had been frustrated lately due to the lack of growth in his profession. He was seriously contemplating a stint in private security. There was a lot of money there, but to get the big bucks, you need to have some chops, he always said. She believed it meant a reputation of some sort. She put the cups down on the side stool and gently stroked his hair. She let her saree fall carelessly off her chest in case Rachit wanted to de-stress himself first thing in the morning.

"Rachit… get up, baba… it's 8 already." The voice was more loving than usual. Sultry even.

Kamble was a light sleeper, and he hardly slept the night because of the impending IGP meeting. He opened his eyes to the beautiful sight of his wife's inviting demeanour. He thanked his stars and pulled her into the bed with one swift motion. He avoided kissing Rashmi and snuggled her neck instead. She smelled like… peace. Her scent instantly calmed his anxieties and aroused his desires. His one hand explored and squeezed her, and the other hand went south for exploration.

"Aren't you getting late, Kamble Saheb?" Rashmi threw the cliché.

"I may be a little late, but you are right on time, *meri jaan*." Cliché begets cliché.

Rashmi ensured she was ready to receive and accommodate him, and Kamble didn't make her wait. The couple started their day with glory. Mutual glory, actually. Kamble was looking at her lovingly as she acted genuinely coy and bashful.

"Now, c'mon, get ready… *chalo*…" she sat up and started adjusting with her back towards him.

He grabbed her from behind. "I am ready… now… for anything."

It ended the way it all started. Cliché.

NEEL

It was a usual morning in Clarence House. Amma and Ibu had gone for a walk as promised. Deva was tending his garden, and Shiksha was en route to Neel's room with her chai and his coffee. She knew he slept late because she didn't sleep at all. She could hear him walking, the electric kettle hissing, and noodling of the guitar; he was probably up till 3. She didn't disturb him. She wanted to, but she was busy. She was busy savouring the fact that Neel was jealous. He said it last night. He was jealous that some other guy was checking her out. He was jealous that she smiled back at the admirer. How cute is that? Neel Mantri… Jealous!!! Is it time to say the unsaid out loud now? She wondered.

She fired the laptop screen. Multiple tabs were open with theories about death by blunt force trauma. She quickly shut the flap down. Not ready for gore this early in the morning.

"No gore this early in the morning… huh?" Neel turned around and yawned with a loud exhale.

"You know what… you… over smart… idiot… that was so obvious… that… it doesn't even deserve a discussion. Your coffee is with me. Come out on the terrace." Shiksha fired a parting shot.

Neel put on his morning costume and almost jogged out to sit next to Shiksha with a thud.

"Damn… you don't need more caffeine, dude! Why are you so amped up already…?"

Neel took out a cigarette, and with a sideways glance followed by an upward nod and Shiksha's smile, he had confirmed that it was safe to light up. So, he did. Shiksha noticed he had been clearly more energetic and present for the last few days.

"How does it work, *yaar*, Neel… from drinking and smoking up every night to researching all night on caffeine… just like that!" Shiksha snapped her fingers for effect.

Neel was nodding as he exhaled a thick stream and took a big gulp. It was as if he was solving a complex differential equation in his mind. Satisfied, he spoke.

"I have very selectively cared for what medical science says, Shiksha. I strongly believe in the power of the mind. The non-existent organ of our body. People often confuse it with the brain. No. Not the brain. Mind. The reason someone is better than his/her peers. The reason someone is 'special.' It's all mind. Now, the mind develops or can be developed over time with will, intent, and, above all, action. But some people are born with a hyperactive, over-hungry mind. The ones you call genius or prodigy."

Neel took a pause as if waiting for Shiksha to point at him at the mention of the word "genius" or "prodigy." She didn't. She had a resting smile. He continued.

"So, the curse of a beautiful mind or the price a genius pays is that it doesn't have an OFF switch. It needs fodder all the time, and if you don't have the fodder, then you'd better have some numbing agent. Alcohol. Weed. Drugs. Almost all the time, it's the genius who turns out to be a drug addict or goes cuckoo. I have my dose of drugs… for now. I am sorted… for now."

He took the last drag. He let the moment hang in the background of the bright Mumbai sun and morning chirps.

"Oh my God… so all geniuses are crazy, and you are a genius too… Neel…" Shiksha overacted her surprise.

"I am telling you, Shiksha… My mind and I had a detailed conversation last night. This case is not easy… Do you realise… there is not a single clue or shred of evidence? But I will still solve it because my mind is telling me… *ho jayega*… Something I will excavate… something will present itself… it will happen… it has to happen. And then I will be a famous sleuth. The world's youngest consulting detective, Neel Mantri." Neel stubbed out the cigarette and stood up in excitement as he finished his declaration.

"Hey, Neel… you know you can talk to me about anything… and anytime, right?"

"Of course, I know that, Shiksha." Neel was doing his stretches.

"Hmm… good. *Chalo*… I am off to college." Shiksha got up but turned around right before the staircase. "Please don't ever become a drug addict, Neel."

Kaka

Kamble was seated in the guest chair, rubbing his sweaty hands as IGP Gadhvi was busy checking his phone. Must be counting his money, Kamble thought. He decided to be patient. Finally, with a satisfactory smile, the IGP turned his attention to him.

"Kamble… what are the updates on Eknath Patil's homicide?" That was straight to the point.

Now, there were actually only 2 updates. One was the discovery of Ramesh Chavan behind this urgency, and the second was that this somehow began in January 2011, and the 2 are related. But Kamble had a hunch not to share either one.

"Nothing, Sir. It's a dead end. No motive. No murder weapon. No CCTV footage. No witnesses. Nothing."

"Hmm…" IGP hummed to sound spontaneous. "Take this case file dated from January 2019, 2 years prior to our case. This should help, somehow. There seems to be a connection."

Kamble was pleasantly surprised at the development. Is the IGP actually helping me to solve the case? he thought. What's the catch here? As he was mulling over it, the IGP boomed.

"You will give me updates twice a week. Even if you have an inkling of a suspect, you will immediately report to me. You will keep me in the loop for everything you do about this case… well, cases. Is that understood, Kamble?" IGP was looking dead into his eyes. There was some fear there.

"Yes, Sir. Loud and clear." Kamble got up. He performed his customary salutation. The moment he was outside the room, he fished out his phone and typed a message to the F4 group. It said:

There is a new, unexpected development. Neel, meet me at the coffee shop at Signal. Call me when you are there.

20

NOVEMBER 8ᵀᴴ, 2023

Mumbai, 1:00 PM

As soon as Neel read the message, he finished his routine as fast as he could and rushed to the coffeehouse. There was no time to wait for Gaurang, who was getting done by 2:30 PM at the earliest. Neel could not wait that long. This urgency was communicated to Gau, and Neel received and discarded the disappointment and emotional acceptance. He had been seated at the coffee table for the past 45 minutes, and finally, Kaka entered. As soon as Kamble reached the edge of the table, he slammed the file theatrically, drawing minor attention, and regretted it immediately. He sat down quietly, leaned towards Neel, and instructed him to lean in too.

"I want you to go home and read what this file says, Neel, and more importantly, what it conveys… I mean, the bigger picture. I am absolutely convinced that I am just being used as an exterminator to figure out the hiding spot." Kamble paused. Neel immediately took the opportunity.

"Kaka… you have already read it. Give me specifics, please… what is your first impression? That is your gut talking…." Neel was interrupted.

"A 30-year-old orphan named Joel D'Souza was murdered on January 7th, 2019, with the exact same modus operandi, i.e., a lethal blow to the head with a blunt instrument with protrusions on the business end. No witness. No family. There is no usable CCTV footage because of the carefully chosen blind spot. Dead end. Cold case."

They were interrupted by the waiter who brought a cappuccino for Kaka and an Americano for Neel—his third in the café and fourth since the morning. Neel was on the edge of his seat. He wanted to ask something but decided to let Kaka give the full download first.

"This case was given by… you know who," Kamble was being careful, "fully aware that it would help the current investigation. It was said out loud that the 2 cases have a connection. This clearly means…"

"A. They know both victims had the same killer.

B. They don't know who the killer is, or else why would they need me? And, most importantly,

C. They know the reason… WHY all this is happening…"

Kamble took a big sip. "I mean, look at the nerve… using me blatantly to fish out the suspect and then what, eliminate the danger? I am being given selective information and just being used to smoke out the suspect's name. That's it. Fucking bastards!" He finished the coffee in one go, mistaking it for a drink.

"Kaka… anything interesting on this… Joel guy…?"

"Oh yes… no angel, not even by a long shot. Orphaned and abandoned when he was a week old at the doorsteps of St. Matthew's Orphanage. Grew up there. Always in trouble at school. Violence and petty theft mostly. He was arrested many times but got out on bail courtesy of the orphanage management. Fed up, he was thrown out of the establishment just a second after he turned 18. Then a lot of quiet for a long time, maybe a drifter, and then found dead right in Mumbai in January 2019, hardly 200 metres from the orphanage." Kamble was fumbling through the file, just to check he had not missed anything major. The decibel level of that monologue drew the attention of the entire café.

Neel was just quiet. He wanted Kaka to cool down a bit as he was genuinely and justifiably angry. A couple of minutes of silence did calm Kamble significantly.

"Ok, Neel. I have rambled quite a bit here. Your thoughts…?"

Neel opened his notebook and turned to a fresh new page.

"Ok, Kaka… This is what we know… Eknath and Joel were killed by the same person. Fair assumption?"

Kamble nodded in agreement. He pulled the notebook towards himself, gesturing to Neel that he would write it down. Kamble wanted Neel to just focus on thinking. Neel continued, in a soft tone. *Sotto voce*, as they say.

"Somebody killed 2 people—and Chavan/IGP know it. They don't know who did it, but they do know why. A huge leap, maybe, but a logical deduction from what Mrs. Patil said… maybe… This all… can be traced back to 2010/2011… maybe. A working hypothesis, if you will." Neel was in the zone, and Kamble silently admired how his thought process worked.

"Kaka, what I mean to say is, let's be ahead of them now. Look at the timeline of our theory. 2011… 2019… 2021. The first gap is way too big, isn't it?"

"What are you trying to say, *yaar*...?" Kamble hissed with slight frustration.

"Kaka... There needn't be just 2... I mean, we were fed these 2 cases only; in actuality, there are... I mean, there should be more. There were more, just like there will be more..."

Neel saw the puzzled look on his face.

"Ok... you are saying there could be more cases similar to these... in the same series, so to say...?"

"Yes... I am 100% sure, Kaka." Neel got excited and immediately calmed himself down and continued.

"Two things we should now be doing that I am sure of: one is that we need to excavate all the cold, unsolved cases in Mumbai since 2010/2011 in which the MO/murder weapon is the same. This is paramount, Kaka. I know it would be a lot, but an unsolved case and a distinct murder weapon should considerably narrow down the list. Second, this is a case of vendetta or vigilante justice. I would try to discover any link between the victims. They cannot be random. There has to be a link."

Kamble took out a photocopy of the entire file and handed it over to Neel, then headed straight to the police station with the original. He had a lot of searching to do. Neel had his task cut out completely, and he wanted to do it in his room. Undisturbed. So, he headed home.

In this entire period of 45 minutes of conversation and file exchange, Kamble didn't notice Paul, IGP Gadhvi's driver, was watching and listening to the whole thing. The whole time.

Paul immediately fished out his phone and dialled.

November 8ᵗʜ, 2023
Clarence House, 7:30 PM

It had been over 4 hours. Amma, Ibu, and Deva had come and gone 4 times to convince Neel to eat something but were met with stoic indifference. Neel had read the report 3 times back-to-back, ensuring he didn't miss anything. He jotted down every relevant piece of information in his syntax. He had drawn the crux of the new case file. It read as:

NAME: JOEL SOUZA

AGE: 30

HEIGHT: 5'9"

ADDRESS: St. MATTHEW'S ORPHANAGE, MUMBAI (LAST KNOWN)

DATE OF DEATH: JANUARY 7ᵗʰ, 2019, AT Around MIDNIGHT.

FAMILY: NONE (ORPHAN)

FRIENDS: NONE

EYEWITNESSES: NONE

CCTV FOOTAGE NOTES: NONE - BLINDSPOTS/NON-FUNCTIONING

CAUSE OF DEATH: REPEATED BLUNT FORCE TRAUMA, MAJORLY TO THE BACK OF THE SKULL

PLAUSIBLE MURDER WEAPON: THE WOUND SUGGESTS A HEAVY BAT/HAMMER WITH PROTRUSIONS AT THE BUSINESS END. IT COULD BE BARBED WIRE, METALLIC BEARINGS, OR GEMSTONES.

NOTES: HAD A RAP SHEET - FOUR ARRESTS AS MINOR. NOTHING AFTER 2010.

POCKET: COCAINE, ECSTASY PILLS, CANDIES, AND A SACHET OF MANGO PICKLE.

Both the murders were in January; it couldn't be ignored. Something about the month…? New Year…?
The candies and mango pickle found in Joel's pockets were also noteworthy, but drug addicts are known to have weird munchies, and something tangy is always preferred, Neel observed.

Neel had been searching the web for any plausible digital connection between Eknath and Joel. No result. He had texted Mrs. Patil to ask if the name Joel D'Souza rang any bell, and she had immediately replied in the negative.

Neel knew he was fresh out of ideas for now. He needed to detach. Maybe some food. He realised he had not consumed anything since morning except 6 cups of black coffee. It was time to eat something to kickstart his brain again. Damn you, Biology.

21
DECEMBER 16TH, 1971

Aurangabad, 6:30 PM

The entire government college was in a hostel mess, hovered around the solitary radio. The news of Pakistan surrendering to India had just been announced, and around 300 Indian men with long side-parted hair, mutton chops, and bell-bottoms were screaming at the top of their lungs.

"BHARAT MATA KI JAI!!!"

The wave of national pride was palpable among the youth, and Anand Mohan Mantri, Ibrahim Sheikh, and Balraam Pandit were no exception. The soon-to-graduate trio majored in Physics, English Literature, and Chemistry, respectively. It was a typical December evening. The chilliness in the evening suggested a hot chai with a serving of pakoras, and the trio obliged.

"So, what's your plan going forward... Amma?" Ibu asked while negotiating a hot morsel.

"Me...? I am going to Bombay. I have applied for a teaching assistant position in the science college. They also have a provision that allows me to continue my master's and then later PhD. So a professor's life awaits, and maybe... Aarti..." Amma blushed.

Ibu and Balraam Pandit chuckled.

"What about you, Ibu…?"

"Similar… All roads lead to Delhi, but mine is in the English Literature vehicle. Be a professor and serve the Bard for life, maybe." Ibu summarised.

Their laughter was interrupted by a loud announcement.

"Ae *fakir ki aulaadon*… c'mon, be gone!" said one while the other pushed them away from their seats. Balraam Pandit was about to protest, but Amma and Ibu restrained him. The trio staggered back and made way for the henchmen of a local politician. It took 5 minutes of restraining, but they were able to sway Balraam Pandit from the scene. After 15 minutes of eerie silence, Amma spoke.

"And Pandit Ji… what are your plans?"

"I just want to be rich and powerful," Pandit announced.

22
NOVEMBER 8ᵗʰ, 2023

Clarence House, 8:00 PM

Neel entered the dining area and was welcomed with a huge cheer from all 4 remaining members of the clan. Amma, Ibu, and Shiksha were breaking bread, and Deva was in and out of the kitchen with garam rotis. Shiksha gestured for Neel to come and sit next to her.

"You look emaciated, yaar, Neel…. Have you eaten anything at all…?" She was pissed.

"Haan haan… of course," Neel lied and was called out by Deva from the kitchen.

"LIAR… Neel Baba is a LIAR!"

Shiksha fixed a plate all the while staring at him. No opposition. No comments. Like an obedient child, he began eating. But he was lost, stuck, irritated, quiet. It was evident to all of them, and a consensus was reached to make the boy talk.

"You know, the best way to learn is to teach, beta…" Ibu continued. "From what Shiksha tells me, you have made some inroads in the case but not fast enough for your liking… So… why don't you say all the bullet points out loud and see if we can help… maybe…?"

Neel was not amused.

"*Arey*… just jog the details one by one… maybe you… yourself… Neel Mantri can catch something he's missing…" Amma appealed to his inner narcissist. This time, Neel was convinced. Amma winked at Shiksha, who was trying hard not to laugh.

Neel gave a systematic download of every single detail known to him so far in a phased and chronological manner: the 2 victims, Eknath and Joel, and the unknown link between them. The peculiar murder weapon. Every single detail. Everyone was impressed. They were proud, especially of the empathy exhibited and the way he handled Mrs. Patil. The pride in Amma's moist eyes was evident.

"I couldn't understand your theory of **Bheem ki gada**… that mythological weapon being the murder weapon… I mean… not exactly easy to carry or hide… you know…" said Ibu, finishing his raita.

"Ibu… the murders were carefully planned, and definitely, it meant something. To someone. Or a group of people. To the killers or even the victims. This is personal. Not random. Very, very personal, and it all started way back in…"

Amma interrupted Neel's monologue and demanded ice cream.

"When was the last time all of us had dinner together like this, Shiksha…? C'mon, a little scoop, please."

Amma and Ibu retired to the TV room while Shiksha and Neel went back to his room.

"Hey… why don't you look at the case notes while I rest my eyes for 15 minutes. Please wake me up in 15, Shiksha…" Neel couldn't even finish the sentence.

Shiksha just sat there looking at him snore softly. I will not let the world hurt you anymore, Neel, I promise. She kissed his forehead and switched off the light.

November 9ᴛʜ, 2023
Clarence House, 3:30 AM

"So who is this girl I'm hearing you like... what's her name... Sara... huh?"

"It's not Sara, Mom... it's Sarah... with an 'H'... enunciate the 'H,' Mom!"

"Oh... look at this eight-year-old kiddo defending the honour of his girlfriend... Saraaahhhhh..."

"She is not my girlfriend, Mom. We just like each other. She's quite cute, by the way."

"Awww... quite cute... huh... Neel Mantri loves Sarah... Neel loves Sarah... Neel loves Sara..."

Navya Mantri was filled with love for her son. She could see the pinkish hue on Neel's cheeks at the mention of the girl. She could see he was staring outside the car window, watching the rain taper away on the glass, his favourite sight. She could see her boy blossoming into a genius and inheriting her love for books and stories. She could see them spending the whole summer vacation solving puzzles together.

But what she couldn't see was a car speeding towards them, driven by a drunkard on the wrong side. She could see it now. Right in front. She had to save Neel. The collision was inevitable. She threw herself on Neel, completely engulfing him nanoseconds before the impact.

In the hospital, Neel opened his eyes and saw his father and Amma sitting beside him on the bed. His father kissed his forehead and said, "Goodbye, Neel." There was a finality there.

He could feel it. His eyes followed his father, who was going away and never returning. He knew. A man with a broken heart or a coward leaving an eight-year-old behind. Who can say? But what he didn't know was where his Maa was. Or he didn't want to know. His eyes darted to every corner and stopped at Amma's face, which just looked back at him emptily. He knew instantly. The child prodigy in him had gauged that he would never meet his Maa again. He would never hear her mispronounce Sara again. He cried, howled, and screamed at the top of his lungs, but there was no voice. He didn't want to scream loud. He didn't want to cry loud. He didn't want to say anything to anyone because the most important part of his being was gone. His voice was gone. His world. His Maa.

At that moment, eight-year-old Neel Mantri just refused to speak. At all.

But the freshly 21-year-old Neel woke up with a shriek… "Maaaaaaaaaaaaaaaa……….!!!"

The same dream. Not a dream, actually. His reality has been haunting his dreams for the last 13 years. Neel wiped his face and saw the time. 3:30…!!! "Shikshaaa…!!!!"

He saw the case files on the table. He didn't feel like looking at them right now. Why not? Why didn't he want to solve the puzzle? Because he wanted to drink.

He was craving alcohol. He was craving weed. He was craving that numbness, that beautiful numbness that comes along with it.

But… what about the mind then? Fuck the mind? Just one drink… maybe 2. Just enough to get numb. And then… the case files…

Neel closed his eyes and started breathing deeply.

After a couple of minutes, he was near the electric kettle, fixing a strong cup of black coffee for himself. Coffee and cigarettes should do. For now. Plus, how sweet the drink would be once he solved the case.

Neel was sitting on the terrace, nursing his cigarette and coffee. No material was required. Whatever info he had, he knew it inside and out.

There was no connection whatsoever between the 2 victims. But he had eerie feelings about the 2 dates of the murders. He wrote them down side by side, slowly jogging his mind for a pattern.

JOEL D'SOUZA | EKNATH PATIL

Jan 7th, 2019 | Jan 19th, 2021

Why did these dates look familiar to him? He had seen them somewhere before, not individually, but together. He remembered these dates being special in a totally different context.

And like lightning striking, Neel remembered where he had seen the dates together. He quickly verified it on the search engine and found that he was right.

What? No… it doesn't make sense. He would have just brushed it aside as a coincidence if he believed in coincidences even slightly.

He had celebrated these dates. What could be the connection?

While he was racking his brain, a notification popped up about a new message in F4 from Kaka.

Found 6 more similar cases between 2010/11 until now. 3 of them match the MO exactly. Meet me at the coffee house at 11:00 AM.

23
NOVEMBER 9TH, 2023

09:30 AM

The lazy morning observed the quick back-to-back conversations in the F4 group.

Gau

I can't believe you guys are meeting again without me today. Why can't all this be done after college!!! 😣

Shiksha

Awww… *bechara* Gaurang… 😌

Gau

Shuuuuut uuppp… Shiksha…

Shiksha

Awwwwwwww……

Gau

Feeling abandoned big time… 😣

Shiksha

Let's meet in the evening, and we will catch up soon. Come to Clarence House.

Gau

Ok….lemme confirm… I have a busy day. Submissions are on.

Shiksha

Cool. Let me know.

Neel

Shut the fuck up, guys!!!!
Kaka has left the group.

Neel

I told you… idiots! 😡
Kaka has joined the group

Neel

Sorry, Kaka. Never again. Please 🙏

Gau

Sorry, Kaka. Never again. Please 🙏

Shiksha

Sorry, Kaka. Never again. Please 🙏

NOVEMBER 9ᵀᴴ, 2023
Coffee House, 11:00 AM

"Here…" Kamble gently patted 6 duplicate files on the table as soon as he entered the coffee house and took a seat with his back to the door. As expected, Neel had been waiting there since 10:00. Neel had already decided not to share his observation regarding the pattern he discovered between the murder dates for now. He wanted to see if the argument held any water and if it was really a pattern. It was just too weird to be true. So he decided to keep it to himself for now. Who knows, it really could be a coincidence.

"Six unsolved cold cases starting all the way from 2011. Mumbai jurisdiction. Blunt force trauma to the head. Murder weapon in the ballpark of our MO." Kamble jotted down the salient points.

"Ballpark… Kaka?"

"Three of them match exactly. The murder weapon is a heavy instrument with protrusions on the business end. The other 3 are just blunt hits on the head, but…" Kamble immediately noticed IGP's driver, Paul, standing outside the window and smoking, clearly attempting to eavesdrop and remain unseen. Was he being tracked? Was IGP ensuring he was shadowed?

Kamble was a good cop. He knew this was not a coincidence…

He immediately gestured for Neel to be quiet and suggested an outside presence with his neck and eyes, pointing to the window corner. Neel didn't fully understand but kept quiet.

"Chal, Neel…" Kamble got up and announced loudly. "Arey, if you want any other help for your college research, let me know. And next time, come to the station naa… don't be scared."

Kamble faked a laugh, made a *I will call you later* gesture, and left the place. Neel was comprehending the gravity of it now. Someone was really and rightfully spooked.

November 9ᵗʰ, 2023
Clarence House, 2:00 PM

Neel reached home, still coming to terms with the fact that someone was watching them in the coffee house. He was excited. Such movie-like thrill. That's what he wanted from life. Thrill. Action. Mystery. Neel rushed to his room, requesting Deva for a sandwich and a coffee. Amma and Ibu were having their siesta. Neel put his phone on silent and got to work. He started consuming the file content slowly and methodically, making notes side by side.

6:00 PM

Four hours, one sandwich, and 4 cups of coffee later, Neel had his notes ready. Kamble Kaka was right, actually. Three of the 6 files didn't quite fit the pattern. The cause of death could have been a hit from any instrument. Just because they were unsolved cases didn't mean they qualified. So, he took the bold guesstimate and set them aside. The synopsis of the other 3 relevant cases in order of recency was…

#3

NAME: RAJEEV TIWARI

AGE: 45

HEIGHT: 5'9

ADDRESS: JAWAHAR NAGAR, BORIVLI - W

DATE OF DEATH: JUNE 23rd, 2013, AT around MIDNIGHT.

FAMILY: WIFE & 2 KIDS BACK IN THE VILLAGE. NEVER VISITED MUMBAI.

FRIENDS: ALL QUESTIONED WITH WATERTIGHT ALIBIS.

EYEWITNESSES: NONE

CCTV FOOTAGE NOTES: NONE - BLINDSPOTS/NON-FUNCTIONING

CAUSE OF DEATH: REPEATED BLUNT FORCE TRAUMA, MAJORLY TO THE BACK OF THE SKULL

PLAUSIBLE MURDER WEAPON: THE WOUND SUGGESTS A HEAVY BAT/HAMMER WITH PROTRUSIONS AT THE BUSINESS END. IT COULD BE BARBED WIRE, METALLIC BEARINGS, OR GEMSTONES.

NOTES: SMALL BUSINESS OWNER. REAL ESTATE AGENT.

POCKET: D/L. CASH. A LOT OF TIN SHAVINGS WERE FOUND STUFFED IN POCKETS.

#2

NAME: JUNAID AKHTAR

AGE: 48

HEIGHT: 5'6"

ADDRESS: TULSIWADI, KURLA - E

DATE OF DEATH: MARCH 16th**, 2012,** AT around MIDNIGHT.

FAMILY: WIDOWER WITH NO KIDS. 2 BROTHERS. NEXT DOOR NEIGHBOURS.

FRIENDS: ALL WITH ALIBIS.

EYEWITNESSES: NONE

CCTV FOOTAGE NOTES: NONE - BLINDSPOTS/NON-FUNCTIONING

CAUSE OF DEATH: REPEATED BLUNT FORCE TRAUMA, MAJORLY TO THE BACK OF THE SKULL

PLAUSIBLE MURDER WEAPON: THE WOUND SUGGESTS A HEAVY BAT/HAMMER WITH PROTRUSIONS AT THE BUSINESS END. IT COULD BE BARBED WIRE, METALLIC BEARINGS, OR GEMSTONES.

NOTES: HAD A RAP SHEET - ONE ARREST AS A MINOR. DEALT IN SCRAP TRADING.

POCKET: IDENTIFICATION, CASH. BODY WAS FOUND CLAD IN A BLANKET.

#1

NAME: VINAYAK GATAK

AGE: 50

HEIGHT: 5'6"

ADDRESS: TARDEO, MUMBAI

DATE OF DEATH: APRIL 3rd, 2011, AT around MIDNIGHT.

FAMILY: NONE

FRIENDS: ALL WITH ALIBIS.

EYEWITNESSES: NONE

CCTV FOOTAGE NOTES: NONE - BLINDSPOTS/NON-FUNCTIONING

CAUSE OF DEATH: REPEATED BLUNT FORCE TRAUMA, MAJORLY TO THE BACK OF THE SKULL

PLAUSIBLE MURDER WEAPON: THE WOUND SUGGESTS A HEAVY BAT/HAMMER WITH PROTRUSIONS AT THE BUSINESS END. IT COULD BE BARBED WIRE, METALLIC BEARINGS, OR GEMSTONES.

NOTES: HAD A RAP SHEET - EIGHT ARRESTS. MAJOR POLITICAL WORK.

POCKET: D/L. CASH. RIGHT THUMB WAS SLICED OFF CLEAN DURING STRUGGLE.

Neel admitted there was enough information on the table now. It was time to go micro. Something caught his attention. He was looking at the missing right thumb of victim #1, Vinayak Gatak. And then he saw all the 5 victims' reports at the same time. Bingo!!!!!

Why hadn't he seen that before? It was right there.

There was a pattern. His phone buzzed. There was a text message from Kaka.

"I will come to Clarence House tonight. Haven't seen Amma in long. Will discuss the details there. Also, tell Deva I will eat there."

24.
November 9th, 2023

Clarence House, 9:30 PM

The beautiful second-floor terrace of Clarence House was bracing itself for the very first non-alcoholic *mehfil* in decades. Neel had already informed Shiksha and Deva that Kaka was coming to visit. Because of the current policy of Clarence House, as per Shiksha's diktat, tonight was going to be dry, and the septuagenarian twins were cool with it. No revolt. To reward this obedience from the senior citizens, the menu had prawns and fish curry with a surprise at the end: **Moong Dal Halwa**. Shiksha was satisfied with the aroma galore in the kitchen. Plus, a Deva thumbs-up was the biggest certification for any gastronomic experiment for her. She went out to join the boys, who were extra ravenous for food tonight, given the lack of fluids to wash it down. As expected, Amma, Ibu, and Kamble Kaka were reminiscing while Neel Mantri was quietly sitting in one corner, waiting for the discussion to graze towards the investigation.

"How are the butter garlic prawns, gents?" Shiksha parked herself next to Neel.

"Awesome, Shiksha… beautiful garlic flavour… these crusty crustaceans are yum!" chirped Kaka.

"Kya re Kamble… you were so angry when you came, and now look at you… crusty crustaceans… nice alliteration, Kamble Kaka… Why don't you thank Ms. Shiksha Sheikh…?" Amma was laughing at his own joke. Only him.

"It's the food, Amma… the love… the company. My job makes me meet the scum of the Earth on a daily… almost hourly basis. On top of it, the corrupt cops are worse and more crass than the criminals. Believe me. It gets to me. I loved Physics. I loved your lectures. I wanted to be you, Amma… But…" Kamble stopped for another prawn.

"And you were great too…" proud Amma joined in. "He was… is my best student to date. Methodical. Honest to the core. Could have been a great professor."

"So, what happened…?" Neel joined in.

"Life happened…" Kamble threw a cliché. "Baba was in service, and he died on duty. I was a fresh graduate. They offered me a job in the department much higher than the entry level as per government norms, and I took it. For my mother and 3 younger sisters." Kamble finished the cliché.

"But all your obligations are over now, Kamble, so what is stopping you from pursuing higher studies…?" asked Ibu, perfectly knowing the answer.

"My kids, Ibu… what else… their studies, their tuitions, their clothes, their cell phones, their data packs, their sleepover pizza parties, and then finally college fees… should I go on?" Kamble was shaking his head, and the retired men were laughing.

"Ok, ok… enough bitching from grown-up men. Now, come to the dining table. Fish curry and rice followed by Moong Dal Halwa." Shiksha winked at the oldies, who were just jumping like toddlers.

After the sumptuous fish curry, piping hot halwa was being hogged by everyone on the terrace except Neel. He was busy setting up a white sheet as a screen on the vacant wall to project his findings from his portable mini-projector. He set up the apparatus and ran it through. Successfully. He was ready now.

"Ok everyone, especially Kaka… I want your attention, please." All of them turned to face him standing next to the screen with a pointer.

Neel began his presentation. His notes on Eknath Patil were on the screen.

"When Kaka first introduced this case to me, there was one victim. No motive. No murder weapon. Next slide. This is Joel D'Costa. The second case, with almost an unsaid guarantee, is related to the first one. How, though? No idea. No motive. No murder weapon."

Everyone was listening with rapt attention and nodding along.

"Now, this is the hand Kaka and I were dealt with. I didn't want to take liberties here, but we were playing a rigged game. Kaka… please share… only if you want to…"

Kamble was done with his dessert and already had his game face on.

"A politician in power and a corrupt cop at the top," he began. "I was being played. I was only processing what was selectively being fed to me. But Neel read between the lines. Because of him, we now know more than we should. And the best part is, they don't know that we know."

Neel noticed that Kaka didn't reveal Ramesh Chavan or IGP Gadhvi's names. He also chose not to reveal and go against his partner. He took the baton back from Kamble.

"We added 3 new victims to our list purely based on the working hypothesis that… well, there have to be more victims… and… They all have one thing in common. The modus operandi of murder, which entails - the mysterious murder weapon, no witnesses, no CCTV, well planned." Neel flashed the notes of 3 other victims one by one.

"Now, here is my analysis. Three points. Number 1…."

"The fountainhead of this saga, the origin, is somewhere around 2010/2011. No proof yet."

Amma and Ibu looked at each other and then at Kamble, who nodded affirmatively.

Neel was walking and talking. In the zone. Decisive. Shiksha was proud. Everybody, including her, was glued.

"Number 2… All 5 of them had the same murder weapon. Some kind of customised tool for revenge. Like a Bheem ki Gada, for example. The point is - it's personal. No proof yet." He was getting louder.

"No proof yet and no proof yet… Neel Mantri… Hypotheses need to be proven. It is a basic scientific principle." It was Amma, echoed by Ibu. Neel smiled and projected a final slide.

"Look at this list. It just contains 3 details of our victims. Name, date of murder, and one peculiar thing which was found on or nearby them." It read:

#1 VINAYAK GATAK
April 3rd, 2011
The thumb of the right hand was sliced off clean.

#2 JUNAID AKHTAR
March 16th, 2012
The body was wrapped in a blanket.

#3 RAJEEV TIWARI
June 23rd, 2013
Tin fillings or shavings were stuffed in the pockets.

#4 JOEL SOUZA
January 7th, 2019
Cocaine, weed, candies, and a mango pickle sachet were found in the pocket.

#5 EKNATH PATIL
June 8th, 2021
RD Burman CD was found nearby.

"Let me start with RD Burman. Pancham da, as he was fondly called. Pancham means 5, and he was victim number 5." Kamble and Shiksha had their jaws on the floor. Amma and Ibu were on the edge of their seats now. Neel was getting warmed up.

"Mango pickle… the Hindi word for pickle is *achar*… colloquially almost *CHAAR* and we have victim no. 4!"

"Neel… what the fuck… how?!" Kamble was jumping in his seat. Quite literally.

"Wait, Kaka… wait… There's more… Vinayak had his thumb sliced off. It was a direct reference to the famous mythological character of Eklavya… Ek… victim number 1!"

"Wooooooooow…" That was synchronised.

"Tin fillings… tin… in Hindi… it is called…."

"Teeeeeeeen… Number 3!!!!" The crowd was animated now.

"What about number 2, Neel?" Kamble couldn't get enough.

Neel was walking slowly, taking in the applause, basking in the glory. After all the high-fives, the crowd settled down. It was time to explain the observation. Everybody was glued to their seats and focused on Neel, except Shiksha. She was lost in her thoughts.

"Amma… you remember the case of the Dancing Men in the Sherlock Holmes series. That line was said by Sherlock. That beautiful line was written by Sir Arthur." Amma nodded sideways. Anyway, the question was rhetorical. Neel continued.

"It said… What one man can invent, another can discover. From the beginning, because of the complexity of the murder weapon, it was obvious that the murder was premeditated. But over time, I was sure that it was all personal. Vendetta. Revenge. Vigilante justice, if you will. So there had to be a signature. A subliminal message. There is a bigger story at play here." He let his words hang in the air.

"Someone is on a mission and keeping score. We have 5 till now… In order to figure out how many more to go, we need to trace the origin… WHY it all began, and that's what I am going to focus on." Neel took a bow.

Applause again. "What about number 2… Neel?" Kamble repeated his question.

"I don't know, Kaka… I can't search for the evidence. I am racking my brain to figure out how wrapping the body in a blanket ties to number 2, but I am sure it does… it has to… right? This all can't be just a coincidence." Neel finally sat down.

"Well, no worries… you are on the right track. *Chalo*… let's call it a night. I have a feeling we have a lot of work on our hands. Good night, Amma. Good night, everyone." Kamble signed off.

Everyone was scattering and winding up.

"Dohar," a voice boomed. It was Shiksha.

One of the Hindi translations for a blanket would be *dohar*… DOhar… giving a DO, which means 2… and that's victim #2. Good night, everyone." Shiksha logged out.

25
December 25ᵀᴴ, 1973

Mumbai, 9:00 PM

The trio were celebrating Christmas at the newly acquired dream house of Anand Mohan Mantri. This beautiful three-floor establishment was arranged on a 99-year lease by Amma's father-in-law. The property was Victorian, beautiful, and cheap. It was so cheap that even Amma's self-respect allowed it. After all, he was paying rent, no matter how minuscule it was. His wife, Aarti, was on the first floor catering to guests, while the trio was catching up on the second-floor terrace.

"What is the deal with the name CLARENCE HOUSE? I mean, what is the connection here?" Ibu was curious.

"I didn't name it. I mean, I didn't rename it. This house was built around independence and was named by the first owner. I am just respecting the legacy. It is a piece of history… why change it? Anyway… it is a huge house with 3 habitable floors. I am currently using the whole house, but if you 2 want to move in with your families, it would be… what's the word… Utopian!" Amma was smiling at the possibility.

"Nahi yaar, Amma… I am happy in Delhi. But someday… I feel we all should live together here like hostel days. Maybe after retirement. What say, pandit?" Ibu finished his drink.

"Let's see… right now, I don't have time to even dream. My chemical factory in Alibaug is all set. It's up and running in 15 days. You see, guys, I will make so much money. You will see…" Pandit confessed.

"What will you do with so much money, yaar Pandit…?" the duo echoed in unison.

"Live it up. Do not get bullied by rich assholes. It would be a life of power and dignity." Pandit made it crystal clear.

"Ohooo yaar, Pandit… Anyways, have you guys seen Bobby?… That Dimple Kapadia is a dream yaar… I mean, talk about sexy…" Ibu interjected.

Suddenly, the trio forgot about everything they were discussing and, for a moment, had a common thought or image: Dimple Kapadia. The chain of thought was broken by the sound of crockery being set on the table.

"Dinner time, boys," announced Aarti, who was supervising, and a younger guy was following her instructions.

"Arey waah bhabhi. Thank you. What an aroma." Both Ibu and Pandit were literally salivating.

"Suno Anand… please manage na. I would go and handle the other guests. Ibu… Pandit bhaiya… enjoy your favourite food. Ok, bye."

Amma stood up next to the younger guy and put his hand on his shoulder.

"Boys… this gentleman right here embodies loyalty, respect, and unmatched cooking talent. He is Aarti's cousin from the maternal side and is going to live with us from here on. The more, the merrier. Please welcome Deva!"

26

NOVEMBER 10TH, 2023

Clarence House, 9:00 AM

Shiksha woke up insanely jealous. Not jealous. More like pissed. Everybody was already up and running. Amma and Ibu were back from their walk. Deva had tended to his garden. And this night owl Neel Mantri—even he was up. And the worst part—all were sitting at the dining table having their own favourite version of chai/coffee… without her. No one bothered to wake me up, she thought. Well, she should say it out loud.

"No one bothered to wake me up," muttered Shiksha as she took her chai from Deva.

"Ohoo… how rarely you sleep through the morning, *beta*. We let you enjoy it," Ibu gave a standard reply, buried in the newspaper.

They won't get it. She liked that all her boys were dependent on her for their choice of morning brew. She liked that dependency. She liked to softly crib about that dependence every morning. It's so simple. What is there not to understand here? But she kept quiet.

"So what next, Neel… I mean, what comes next… in your case?" inquired Ibu.

"It has to be the search for the origin—where it all began. There are so many unanswered questions right now. It would be foolish to try and search for individual answers. I would rather look for WHY… Why has this all happened… and somehow, I think it all traces back to…"

Neel was interrupted by an excited child called Anand Mohan Mantri.

"Hey, Neel… can we continue our discussion on the cricket rink… What say… hit a few!"

It was hard to say NO to Amma's childlike enthusiasm. Neel gave Amma a double thumbs-up, and the duo headed downstairs to the rink.

"Wait… I am also coming," rushed Shiksha. Ibu couldn't bother less.

Amma took his leg stump guard. Neel took out both the bags of cricket balls—the one with old cherries and the one with new. Neel fished one ball out of the old bag and remembered the last session; it was out of shape. One blue netted bag usually contained 12-15 balls, stored like oranges in a juice shop.

"Check this… does it look ok to you?" Neel tossed the ball to Shiksha, who caught it with one hand, and after a bit of showboating, began to examine it.

"What's the matter, Neel… again bitching about the old balls?" Amma sledged.

Neel ignored the sledge. "Amma… I remember we bought this new bag of balls on the morning of the World Test Championship final, i.e., June 7th, 2023. And I distinctly remember buying this old one here a week before the first pandemic lockdown at the national level."

"So what yaar Neel… c'mon, bowl naa… I am not getting any younger here…" Amma was getting impatient.

"But seriously… we did not play for the entire pandemic, and then once it was over, we had hardly 2 sessions with spin bowling. These balls are really out of shape for the amount of knocking we have done. Plus, the lacquer is almost intact, but the shape is distorted. Weird." Neel was contemplating.

"It's the heat, my friend." Shiksha was done with her analysis. "Lack of hitting, but constant exposure to this crazy Mumbai heat for more than 3 years—what do you expect? And you answered yourself, Neel, that is why the shine or lacquer is intact, but the shape is bent. Heat, my friend. Ain't global warming a bitch." She took a stride and bowled a standard offie.

Amma blocked it perfectly while laughing out loud.

Neel walked up to his mark for a leg spinner. "All I am saying is that… Amma… your mediocre defence is looking better because the ball is not ideal." Neel tossed it up with extra revolutions.

"Now you are talking, my boy. Get your sledge on." Amma chuckled as he blocked it perfectly.

27

November 10ᵀᴴ, 2023

Police Station - Andheri, 10:00 AM

IGP Gadhvi was a cockroach. Everybody knew that, including him. It meant he was an expert in survival. A cockroach can actually leap and fly, but it doesn't do so all the time simply because it doesn't want us to know. It only shows this skill when it is absolutely required. That's why the cockroach survives. Always. His driver Paul had told him about that boy Neel with whom Kamble was discussing the case. Why though? How can that Generation Z tween help Kamble? Why did he involve that boy? But it was not time to confront Kamble simply because it was not required right now. What was urgent was to get the suspect list and get Chavan off his back. That is why the hair on the back of his neck stood up when he got a call from the Khandala police station 15 minutes ago on the official landline.

Khandala was a small hill station on the outskirts of Mumbai, around maybe 100 km out, famous for its bungalows. In the old times, many public servants and army personnel used to choose Khandala to live out their sunset years.

The call mentioned something about a bungalow called Hill Crest at the foot of Tiger Hills in Khandala. It belonged to a retired Colonel Purie, who had owned the bungalow since 2003. In fact, he had it constructed in 2003 after his retirement on a piece of land procured by him in the late 80s. So far, the story checked out for Gadhvi. He had already made some calls to the local registrar's office to corroborate these details. All names and timelines checked out.

Now, Col. Purie had died last week after a long battle with cancer. His son Aashish, who is a US resident, was in town for the last rites, and yesterday, during the cleaning of the bungalow, he came across a small basement room that had a state-of-the-art locking system. The lock was somehow cracked, and he found an elaborate picture collage of a few people, which looked like surveillance, and many copies of police case files. Gadhvi replayed the detailed conversation he had with the inspector, who was already nervous about speaking with an IGP. An exact picture of the event was forming in his cunning brain. So far, so good. So now, Aashish Purie, as he should have, informed the local police station, and an officer came and checked it out. As most of the case files were from the Andheri area, the officer decided to call the IGP office in Andheri. The room is sealed now, and local police are waiting for a team from Mumbai. Aashish Purie flies out to the USA tomorrow afternoon.

Gadhvi believed in luck, destiny, fate, horoscopes, you name it. His gut was telling him that the Gods were ready to smile upon him as they had been for the last 12-13 years. Retired Army Colonel. A bungalow in the middle of nowhere. Only resident. Dead now. A basement with a modern state-of-the-art locking system. Surveillance pictures and case files. It all pointed towards serendipity. Success on a platter with a nice cherry on top.

He summarised all the details of this new development in a message to Ramesh Chavan. First things first. Then he picked up the phone and called Kamble in.

Gadhvi told the entire story to Kamble, with obvious instructions to head to Khandala with a team and take charge. Kamble could feel the excitement in his senior's voice, who was discounting the possibility of a big break. Gadhvi didn't mention the boy, and Kamble didn't mention Paul following him because suddenly, there was another more important elephant in the room.

In 15 minutes, Kamble was en route to the bungalow Hill Crest to find what was waiting there.

November 10th, 2023
Khandala, 1:00 PM

Hill Crest turned out to be quite an iconic address. Kamble was able to locate it very easily. Kamble's inner monologue was switched on as the drive was coming to an end. Every time one drives to Khandala, which is just 100 km out of Mumbai limits, the first thought that comes to mind is how close and underrated this place is. Why doesn't one drive out often to spend a day in the natural beauty on offer here? The answer was an obvious one. Because it was easily available. No planning was required. No long travel. Something so easily available can't be worth it.

One look at the bungalow, and it could be easily assessed that it reeked of affluence and privilege. Kamble knew the details already. The deceased was a retired Colonel. Military. Be careful. The son is an investment banker and a Wall Street suit. Rich. Be very careful. On top of that, Mr. Aashish Purie was a US citizen. Be extremely careful.

Kamble led his team inside the gate and was greeted by a local cop in charge and a handsome middle-aged dashing man with salt-and-pepper hair and beard. Immaculately dressed with a shining Rolex clearly visible. Kamble was sure that Aashish Purie had more money on his person right now than Kamble had in his savings account. Just… be careful. After the formalities of the charge transfer were done, the local cop left. A butler came in with some tea for the cops and some dark purple liquid for the American. Kamble didn't even bother to ask.

"I am sorry for your loss, Mr. Aashish." Kamble felt it would be right to start with extending condolences.

"Thank you. I appreciate it," came the reply with an accent. The constables with Kamble were gawking at the debonair gentleman who spoke weirdly.

"As per my information, there is a basement…." Kamble steered to the point and was interrupted by an even more impatient Aashish.

"Yes… let me show you. Follow me, gents."

As we were walking through the hall, every guest was admiring the tasteful decor. The sight of the swimming pool drew a collective albeit an inaudible sigh.

"Officer, I have to assert again…I have a flight back to the States early tomorrow morning, which I absolutely cannot miss. Could you please accommodate that?" Kamble knew it was not a request. It was uttered with the confidence of a US citizen. Aashish entered a 12-character alphanumeric password into the dashboard of what looked like an ultra-modern security system.

"My father had the password in the will. Can you imagine my surprise…."With an expensive hissing sound, the door to the basement opened.

The scene inside was straight out of a movie. Aashish switched on the light, and the movie came to life. There was an order in the chaos emanating from the room. All the boxes were ticked. There were surveillance photographs of all 5 victims in Kamble's file. A copy of their driver's licences was on a board with numbers attached from 1 to 5. Surveillance pictures were actually dated right from January 2011 to January 2021.

This was information overload for Kamble. The feeling of finding a question paper along with all the answers a day before the exam. This was serendipity. Nothing short of a miracle. Once Kamble understood the reality of what he was seeing, he got to work. He instructed his deputy to arrange for 6 separate boxes, each with a name. It went

#1 VINAYAK GATAK
April 3rd, 2011

#2 JUNAID AKHTAR
March 16th, 2012

#3 RAJEEV TIWARI
June 23rd, 2013

#4 JOEL D'SOUZA
January 7th, 2019

#5 EKNATH PATIL
June 8th, 2021

#6 NEW

The idea was very simple. Sift through every inch of the room and sort the information into the relevant boxes. The surveillance was extremely detailed. Except for the first 2 victims, Vinayak and Junaid, the rest were monitored for years. The cop instinct had taught Kamble to be suspicious all the time with all of it, but such details of all victims were reassuring that it was the right place. Obviously, now the most important box is #6 - NEW. The entries up till now were the diagnostic reports of Col. Purie. Apparently, the cancer diagnosis first appeared around 2014. There were maps of the local region of Mumbai - suburbs, outskirts, etc. Treatment reports and frequent consultation reports revealed the various stages of chemotherapy Colonel was in. Apparently, there was never a chance of recovery, and a slow and painful death was imminent. Kamble knew that a certain death could incentivise a steely resolve of a person to live off the remaining days with purpose.

There was very little doubt left in Kamble's mind that this mountain of evidence pointed to just one thing only. Colonel Purie was the vigilante who eliminated at least these 5 victims. But Why?

Where is the motive? Could all of this be staged. I mean, it was quite convenient with Colonel being dead now. While the team was busy organising the material, Kamble found Aashish in the open area near the pool.

"Do you know or understand what all this means, Mr. Aashish.?

"I mean…not exactly… It ain't exactly feel like good news, you know," Aashish tried to make light of the situation.

"You are right…Sir….it is quite big…and not in a good way…May I know when did you come back to India recently?"

Aashish grew sombre, contemplating the answer.

"Two days after my father died." He most certainly choked up but continued after regaining composure. "As you must have guessed, Inspector, I am what you call a Wall Street asshole with no time for family. It is such a cliché, but it is true here. And I don't even regret it. But he died alone….absolutely alone. He had been with me in the States for an extended period of time in the last 10-12 years but never agreed to move and settle there. Too much love for his country."

Kamble let that disdainful last line go, as the man was clearly hurting.

There was a silence shared by 2 gentlemen respectfully.

"When was your last India visit, Mr. Aashish…I mean before this…"

"I left almost 30 years ago and returned just now. There was nothing here for me, Inspector. Not then. Not now. I was an only child who lost his mother to an accident at the age of 5. I lost my mother. My father lost interest in life. So, he was more than happy to afford my graduation from the US. He was actually relieved at my decision to graduate abroad, so….I am kind of Shahrukh Khan from Swades, except I don't work for NASA, I don't want to light a bulb here, and most importantly, I have no intention to stay."

Kamble was kind of relieved that Aashish was actually oblivious of the gravity of the situation. And also, all his statements were easily verifiable but something told him it would not be necessary.

"Is there any other basement…or safe place? Anywhere may be….?"

"Ummm…there is a small safe in my father's bedroom. I haven't opened it yet. It must be some valuables or documents. Please come, let me show you."

As the team was busy sifting and sorting material evidence into boxes, Kamble waited for that little safe to open.

Out came a passport, insurance policy and a small box - less than 2 feet long and less than a foot wide. Aashish opened it with genuine surprise. And there it was. A gold-plated hammer with gemstones glued at the blunt end. And a note signed by Col. Purie.

"What……is….that?" Mused Aashish.

Kamble knew in a flash. In fact, he knew it exactly. It was a HEAVY BAT/HAMMER WITH PROTRUSIONS AT THE BUSINESS END. IT COULD BE BARBED WIRE METALLIC BEARINGS OR GEMSTONES.

Kamble had read the case files so many times that the exact words were dancing around his eyes as he was staring at the hammer.

It was the murder weapon.

Kamble picked up the note and unfolded it. It just said 3 words.

"THEY DESERVED IT."

28

November 10ᵗʰ, 2023

Mumbai, 10:30 PM

A sophisticated, beautiful lady friend came out of nowhere to pick up Mr. Aashish Purie. Kamble thought the embrace was a tad bit longer for a platonic friend. And his team agreed with him while grinning from ear to ear. After all the boxes were loaded and the house was sealed for the forensic team due tomorrow, they were headed back to the police station to brief IGP Gadhvi. He insisted on an in-person update. Tonight. He also insisted that Aashish come along and sign off on the custody of evidence. Tonight. It felt as if Gadhvi wanted to close the file almost immediately. Tonight.

Kamble offered Aashish a ride along to Mumbai. But the lady friend's BMW was a better-smelling proposition. He recalled the exact words of the reply.

"Oh no, officer, you go ahead. Sam here is going to drive me to the police station. We are right behind you. And then once I sign off the formalities and you are done with me, I am booked in 4 seasons for the night. Tomorrow after breakfast I fly out to Frisco. So, all sorted."

Rich people just talk differently. They even live in a different world. It is not necessary, but it is important to get rich. Kamble reluctantly agreed to it. He flicked his phone to life. A message in the group F4.

Neel

Are there any updates, Kaka?

IGP Gadhvi had already instructed Kamble to report urgently and let his deputy handle all the paperwork with Aashish Purie. A visibly tired Kamble was sitting as an excited Gadhvi puffed away.

"I know forensics will do their job. I know all evidence collected will be verified. But, prima facie, you think we got him? I mean, is it him… damn it…Was…Was it him?"

"Sir….there is a mountain of evidence which says so, and also, the murder weapon fits the bill. I mean, it all points that way, but ……."

"I know Kamble. I know. Tell me your findings." IGP was impatient.

Kamble narrated every single thing found in the basement. The victim's identities, their surveillance, the cancer diagnosis of Col. Purie and, of course, the murder weapon. Gadhvi was showing a rainbow of expressions. He looked genuinely afraid when the victims were mentioned and genuinely relieved hearing that the Colonel was dead. Kamble saved the best for last.

"There was a note, Sir. It said - THEY DESERVED IT." Kamble used his serious baritone for effect.

Gadhvi went unmistakably pale. There was a long period of 30 seconds in which he was absolutely lost in space. Thinking. Remembering. Extrapolating may be. Kamble was too experienced to miss all this. The expression on Gadhvi's face was that of a close call. A near-death experience. A miraculous save. Thank you, God. He regained composure. He flipped out his phone. He couldn't wait. He typed a message to Ramesh Chavan.

THE CHAPTER IS CLOSED, *Bhau*. REGARDS.

"Finish the investigation as per procedure. And relieve Aashish Purie with an open line of questioning if required. Let the forensics confirm the possibility of the found item being the murder weapon and any DNA, which I highly doubt. In my opinion, this chapter is closed. Dismissed."

Kamble detected something in what Gadhvi just said. A new feeling. Something he had never detected. Was it…. gratitude? He gave a tired salute and left.

All was done. Aashish Purie was relieved. Kamble lit an extremely rare cigarette which he bummed off his constable. The group F4 was staring at him.

Kaka

The case is probably solved. Irrefutable evidence. All victims. Colonel Ved Prakash Purie (retd.). Dead now. No discussions right now.

Neel…I will stop by tomorrow for breakfast.

P.S.….Shiksha…your legendary adrak chai… please.

November 11ᵀᴴ, 2023
Mumbai, 2:30 AM

He had taken every single update from Gadhvi, but Ramesh Chavan refused to be relieved. Who was Colonel Purie? He understood the note - THEY DESERVED IT. Because they did. Gadhvi did. He did, too. But how was that Colonel involved? The pragmatist in him couldn't refute the mountain of evidence, too. But this is life. It shows up when you are busy making plans. He had to be careful. But he always was.

29

NOVEMBER 15TH, 2010

Clarence House, 6:30 PM

It had been almost a week since he last smiled, played, chuckled, and laughed. It had been a week since he read Sherlock Holmes, listened to music, and solved a puzzle. It had been a week since Neel spoke. It was the holiday season, but Clarence House bore a grim countenance. Anand Mohan Mantri had lost his wife, Aarti, a long time back. In fact, the cruellest of coincidence was that when Aarti died, her son, Neel's father, was also 8 years old. The whole house was reeking of contempt at this cruel chronological coincidence.

Deva had been crying and trying for the last week to make Neel say something, anything, but all were met with stoic silence.

Navya Mantri was the only woman of the household - the Queen. And her kingdom included her husband Mohit, who loved her dearly, her son Neel, her father-in-law Amma and her brother cum associate cum house caretaker Deva. It was an understatement to say that Navya was the most loved person in the household. And her favourite was Neel. The beautiful, pure, unadulterated love between a mother and her firstborn son. There couldn't be a better love story or a stronger bond than that.

Neel hadn't asked about his father at all. The last muted goodbye in the hospital was the last anybody had seen of Mohit Mantri. He had never gotten over his mother's death, and the loss of Navya triggered every pain, every misery in his heart. He lost his will. He lost his life. He just got lost. There was no point for him to be there anymore. Nobody understood that. Amma and Deva called this out as selfish cowardice, but Neel understood it. And that too with a heartbreaking maturity. Because he knew how pointless it is to live when you lose the love of your life, Amma and Deva were clueless about what was more heartbreaking – Neel's silence or his maturity.

All neighbours, colleagues, and called well-wishers had already conveyed their condolences to the bereaved family. But Amma was waiting for his real family. The family he chose more than 50 years ago. His friends, comrades, brothers in arms - Ibrahim Sheikh and Balraam Pandit.

The trio always met regularly, drank and broke breads together. They knew what was happening in each other's lives the instant it happened. They were almost never together for Diwali or Eid or Christmas, but no sorrow that had befallen any of the trio was suffered alone, and God knew all of them had their fair share.

Amma lost his wife Aarti in the early 80s when Mohit was just 8 years old. Both Ibu and Pandit came running as soon as they heard. They were in Clarence House for more than 6 months, taking care of inconsolable Mohit. To hell with their work, jobs. If one is in pain, they all are in pain.

They were all very different from each other, but one thing they had in common and which held them together as a steely unit was the pain they had gone through in their lives. The almost identical pains all 3 had been through were an unfortunate coincidence, but it had amplified their empathy for each other at another level. The understanding and communication between them no longer needed any language; empathy was enough. The beginning of the 90s saw Ibu losing Razia to cancer. Amma and Pandit flew to Delhi and practically drugged Ibu to get him to Clarence House to heal. His son was studying in Panchgani boarding school. Pandit used to drive every weekend to get him back to spend some time with his father. This went on for almost a year.

Of the 3, Balraam Pandit was the quiet one. And the richest one. He established his factory in Alibaug. Made millions and lived in a huge bungalow. Alone. Not at night, though. Legend has it that Balraam Pandit, for 20 years, never slept alone in his bed. But he always woke up alone. Money. Virility. Personality. Dark and disturbed aura. Women could not get enough of him, and the feeling was reciprocated. His ravenous appetite was insatiable. Until one day, Pandit fell in love. She was the wife of his factory supervisor. Husband. Wife. One child. A small, happy family. Pandit was a philanderer and a womaniser but a gentleman. The woman never got to know of his feelings. In fact, nobody knew except Amma and Ibu. Besides, there was no point. Married. Mother. Muslim. Talk about odds in favour.

But as the trio shared identical pains, the Muslim woman and her husband lost their lives in a car accident, leaving their 18-year-old son behind. Orphaned. Amma and Ibu rushed to Alibaug to refrain Pandit from drinking himself to death. But he was inconsolable. Directionless. Rudderless. Without a purpose. And Ibu gave him one. He reminded Pandit that the boy was a part of that woman. She shared a soul with that boy who was all alone in this world.

18-year-old and angry. Orphaned. Heartbroken. It was not easy to break through.

Amma and Ibu were amazed at the level of care and patience he showed around the boy. An absolute gentle giant. There were loud, rebellious episodes. Running away from home. Breaking every single crockery. Loud music. Yelling. But Pandit soldiered on because that's what she would have wanted. And one day, the boy cried in his arms. All night. Bawled his guts out. Pandit had broken through. It took another patient year, but the trio was able to convince the boy to accept Balraam Pandit's legal guardianship.

He insisted on keeping his faith. His name. But he wanted to take Pandit as his surname. Legend has it that Pandit cried that day. And that's how Asif Pandit became the son Balraam never had.

Finally, Ibu and Pandit arrived. Not a single word was said. The trio sat in silence. Deva got some tea and joined the trio. Amma asked him without saying anything, and Deva nodded his head in negative and started sobbing with his hands covering his face. Neel still refused to say anything or engage with anyone. Finally, Ibu broke the silence.

"Amma….I will take the entire first floor. I want my privacy." There was a gentle chuckle in the group.

The prophecy of them living together was coming true. On a sad note, though. Someone was climbing up the stairs. Ibu gestured for Deva to be seated.

"That must be Shiksha. She was checking the garden below." In came a beautiful little girl with pigtails and a bashful but confident demeanour. Amma patted her head with love and hope. He gestured for everybody to follow him while he was holding Shiksha's hand and leading them all to Neel's room.

He was sitting on his bed, staring at the wall. Calm. Composed. Quiet. Motionless. Emotionless.

"Look Neel who is here…. it Ibu… Pandit Dada… and… who is this new friend of yours….Shiksha!!!"

No response. Not even eye contact.

There were books neatly arranged on his desk beside an all-set chessboard and some puzzles already solved.

As everyone watched, Shiksha quietly scanned the whole room. In detail. Saw the books. Puzzles. And finally picked up the chessboard and put it in front of Neel. She pulled the chair so that she could be right in front of him across the chessboard.

"I am white." That's all she said as she picked up a white pawn and made her move.

The room was so quiet that everyone's heartbeat was audible. Literally, Neel just gave her a look, positioned himself properly in an alert position and played the black pawn.

The game was afoot, and sobbing oldies just hurried out of the room onto the terrace.

"God bless that angel" Amma wiped his eyes as his heart blessed Shiksha.

"How is Asif doing pandit?" Ibu changed the topic. "Why don't you take the ground floor in this house with Asif, and all of us recreate the hostel days?"

"Oh, c'mon Ibu….this might hamper Pundit's life… or should I say night-life…."Rare laughter followed that cliché joke.

Deva was marvelling at the calming effect the last 15 minutes had on Amma. He was just grateful. He just let the trio be and wondered if this Shiksha girl could make Neel Baba eat something.

"Asif is great, actually. During the whole of his 20s and half his 30s, that boy was travelling the world without taking a dime from me, by the way. I wrote him off as a hippie." Said Pandit while he lit an expensive-looking black cigarette.

"But he took the reins of the factory around 5 years back, turned it around and sold the business 3 times more than it's worth." Pandit offered the cigarette to Ibu, who gladly accepted the offer.

"You sold the business? The house? When?" asked Amma as it was his turn to take a puff.

"No… no…I haven't sold the house. It's a holiday home now. Asif had no interest in living and maintaining that business in Alibaug. So we sold it for a Mammoth profit. He parked the money in diversified investments and a small chunk for his new venture." Pandit lit another one as Amma and Ibu had no intention of passing the joint.

"What new venture…?"

"So I might not take your ground floor, Amma, but I just bought a penthouse 2 km from here. Asif rented a small studio closer to his business while he was building it. And the new venture is a watering hole. A bar."

There was a loud cheer. High fives.

"Pandit living the dream. What is it called?"

"Asif wanted to name it simply and with my name in it. Now, who cares about Pandit's bar? Then we tried Balraam's Bar, but even that was not …you know… cool enough. He wanted a no-nonsense masculine name to go with his worker's drinking place kind of theme."

Pandit stubbed the butt and let out a last satisfying exhale.

"So we settled on Balli's bar."

30

NOVEMBER 11ᵀᴴ, 2023

Clarence House, 8:30 AM

Gaurang was sad, hurt and irritated. He was sad that he lost so much excitement last week in the investigation. Neel was too busy to talk and occupied with his submissions. He was hurt that Neel didn't bother to call him to share or update or just make him a part of the whole thing. He missed the big reveal of the murder counts the other day. Neel didn't call for that either. He wanted to bask in his friend's glory. He was irritated with himself as to why still, after all that, on Saturday morning at half past 8 in the morning, he was standing outside Clarence House. Visiting unannounced. He loved them both. Neel, a little more.

As Gau entered, he first encountered Deva tending to his garden on the ground floor. Pleasantries were exchanged, and he climbed up the stairs, fully prepared to wake the other 2 musketeers up. But to his utter dismay, he found Shiksha and Neel working on their laptops, and by the look of it, they had pulled an all-nighter.

"You just don't miss me… do you?" Gau entered the room and thundered.

Neel acknowledged him barely with an upward neck movement, but Shiksha expressed pleasure.

"Hey Gau…where have you been?" A high 5 was shared.

"Zip it. I will deal with that later. Tell me what has happened.…that text from Kaka.…what does it mean…?"Gau straight away addressed the elephant in the room.

For a moment, it looked as if Neel was about to answer, but he buried himself on the screen.

"That text is all we know. Apparently, some late retd. Col. Purie is the one. Kaka is coming for breakfast, so we will know further. But someone is convinced that Kaka is mistaken……"Shiksha was grinning.

"I didn't say mistaken. I said, misled. We searched everything available on Col. Purie all night. Did you find any connection? No!" Argued Neel.

Gau knew how to hurt Neel, and he really wanted to, so he fired a salvo.

"You are just bitter that you couldn't solve it. That's all, loser."

As Shiksha burst out laughing, Gau ran out of the room, and Neel chased him only to run into Rachit Kamble.

NOVEMBER 11TH, 2023.
Clarence House, 9:30 AM

Overworked and under-slept, Kamble enjoyed the signature ginger tea by Shiksha first. Everyone was patiently waiting for him to relish and finish his brew except Neel. The boy was going through a tornado of emotions inside and brimming with questions, but he managed to keep his exterior calm. Amma and Ibu had just returned from their morning walk and had hardly invested in the drama yet.

"Ok…so here goes. Do not interrupt me till I am completely done. Do you understand?" The warning was fired at the hardy boys - Neel and Gau.

Kamble went through the entire episode chronologically and did not spare any detail. The discovery and call by Aashish to local police, the call to Gadhvi, and the irrefutable evidence of surveillance, identity cards and police case files were mentioned by Kamble quite graphically. And then the climax. Epilogue. Crescendo. The discovery of a potential murder weapon. A gold-plated hammer with gemstones, which prima facie fits the bill. At this point, all eyes, including Kamble's, were focused on Neel, who was absorbing everything with his eyes closed. Kamble spoke non-stop for almost 20 minutes and deservedly took a break for 30 seconds.

He raised his index finger to indicate that he wasn't done. Nobody spoke.

"Now the forensics are at the site as we speak in search of any foreign DNA or any other evidence. The hammer has been sent to the forensic lab here in Andheri. I know many questions are unanswered, but they are most likely to remain that way, with Colonel Purie being dead now. I am done." Kamble finished and gestured to Neel to ask anything he wanted.

Neel took a deep breath while formulating what he wanted to convey.

"You are right, Kaka. The evidence is irrefutable. I mean, surveillance pictures dated more than a decade back are definitely solid evidence. But…"

Kamble stood up instantly.

"No, but…No if….Neel…….I know the questions, and I am trying to find the answers. But unless you convince me otherwise, I am going to go with Occam's razor. Colonel did it."

Gau was too afraid to ask so he nudged Shiksha who mustered the courage given the mood Kamble was in.

"What is Occam's razor Kaka?"

"Loosely translated, it means the most obvious and simple solution is usually the one closest to truth. The Colonel did it." Summarised Amma. And just like that, the meeting was adjourned.

Kamble touched Amma's feet and made a move to leave. He turned around at the door.

"Neel…you have something new and drastic, I am all ears ….but if not ……then……"

NOVEMBER 11ᵀᴴ, 2023.
Clarence House, 11:30 AM

Three twenty-somethings. Three laptops. Saturday morning. Not even in the wildest dream would one guess that the gang is playing sleuth. And that too in a lost cause. Neel put down his system and went deep in thought. Shiksha and Gau followed suit a minute later.

"Oh my God… THE SILENCE…….ughhhh…"Gau broke the silence in the room.

"Neel… what is it? Out with it now… please…"Shiksha leaned back with her hands crossed.

Neel got up and went next to his small whiteboard in the corner. He picked up a black marker and a red one, too.

"Ok, let's lay it all on the proverbial drawing board from the start. *Tabula Rasa!*"

"What tabla… what again…"Gau jumped at the foreign noise.

"Arey… it is Latin for a clean slate. Let's start from the beginning. Shall we…?"

"Then say that naa… poser!" Gau mumbled.

Neel ignored the quip. Not the time.

"We searched every digital footprint Colonel had to offer - news cuttings, Kargil war veteran, limited social media presence but nothing draws blood…right? Let's start over. Can you guys please come here next to the board?" Neel using the word "Please" was rare, so the duo obliged, albeit snickering at each other.

He handed the black marker to Gau and the red one to Shiksha. They were standing on either side of the board facing Neel who was standing right in the front.

"Gau…the black is for the victim's name… or any name for that matter and Shiksha…the red is for time-stamp or date stamp or year stamp in this case…… Ready."

The duo nodded in affirmation.

Neel picked up his notes.

"Gau…just write the initials as I say the names of the victims in chronological order - Vinayak Ghatak, Junaid Akhtar, Rajeev Tiwari, Joel D' Souza and Eknath Patil."

The initials of the victims in black were in a line on the board now.

"Shiksha ….put the date of murders in dd/mm/yy below each initial now……April 3rd, 2011, March 16th, 2012, June 23rd, 2013, January 7th, 2019, and January 19th 2021…"

Shiksha completed the event timeline chart. All 3 were facing the board now.

VG.	JA.	RT.	JD.	EP
03/04/11.	16/03/12.	23/06/13.	07/01/19.	19/01/21

"Ok, let's take a seat, guys. I will say every relevant question out loud, and let's jot down the answers if we find one. If we don't, then obviously, we dig…….Gau, could you please type this all out on a Word document……. Let's go." The excitement in Neel's voice was building again.

Neel was pacing faster now. Shiksha was sitting ramrod straight. Alert. And Gau was ready.

"Why did it all start?" Boomed Neel.

Shiksha and Gau were waiting.

"Because something happened…something big between December 2010 and January 2011….big enough to unleash a revenge spree which has lasted a decade." Neel paused, waiting for the right remark from the duo.

"How do we know that…?"Shiksha volunteered.

"Two plausible hints - Vinayak, our first victim, a political activist and a shady character, was the first to be murdered in April 2011. As per Mrs. Patil, her husband Eknath almost changed overnight and came into a large sum of money around January 2011. So there…sounds convincing enough for a working theory?" Neel was pacing even faster now.

Gau was typing really fast now but still gave a resounding YES with Shiksha.

"Second question - WHAT happened…?"

"We don't know," Came the unanimous answer.

"Third question - WHERE did it happen…?"

"We don't know." Consensus again.

The body language of the group deflated a bit because of 2 noughts. Neel thought for a second and went close to the board again.

"Notice the gap between the third and fourth victim. Six years. Why?"

The group was thinking. Shiksha sprang up.

"Kaka said the cancer diagnosis of Col Purie came in around 2014. Right? Maybe that's why? He was getting his

treatment in order. That, of course, if Col Purie is our guy…
…"She let it hang.

"Definitely makes sense," Gau blurted, and Neel nodded in agreement.

"Next… why such a niche murder weapon?"

Gau knew this one. "The revenge was driven by justice. It was personal. That's why."

There was a long silence now.

"Ok…now what…?" It had to be Gau.

Neel picked up his phone and texted someone, and almost immediately, a reply came, which made him alert.

"Guys…search for the whereabouts or any activity of Col Purie around the end of 2010 and beginning of 2011 somewhere during that time, and comb through his entire digital footprint. Also, this time, let Mr. Aashish Purie, his son, also be part of the investigation." He picked up his wallet and pocketed the phone.

"And you are off to….?" Asked Shiksha.

"I have to meet Mrs. Patil one more time and also go meet the caretaker of Joel Dsouza's orphanage."

"What a shame. It all started when……" mumbled Gau.

Neel was about to leave but stopped short.

"What do you mean… what shame….started when…?"

"Oh, nothing…I mean, on April 3rd 2011…the whole country was busy celebrating our World Cup win during the early hours…and this started….What a shame…"

Neel froze completely. A sudden thought forced him to open his notes again. The moment he saw it, he blurted… ."Fuck…why didn't I put that together."

"What…What is it…?"The remaining duo asked in unison, but it was too late as Neel had literally run out of the room.

31
NOVEMBER 11ᵀᴴ, 2023

Mumbai, 2:30 PM.

IGP Gadhvi was going through a plethora of emotions at the same time. He was waiting outside the office of the man who had made his career, but he deeply wished he had never met that man. The ruthlessness with which the man operated scared Gadhvi to date. He owed everything he owned today to the serendipity of meeting the man and being in the right place at the right time. But a leopard doesn't change its spots. The man was the devil incarnate. Satan. He felt a little relieved, though, that the current ordeal might come to an end and close that evil chapter of the past completely. He was almost sure that it was all done, and he could breathe normally now. He could move on to enjoy again. The finer things in his life. His mistress, first of all. It was a long time now. He was yearning bad. He was getting excited just thinking about it.

"Go in. Saheb will meet you now," announced the pompous P.A. to Satan.

Gadhvi put a temporary stop to the naughty train of thought in his mind for the time being. He entered the plush office and stood next to the table. His designated place, apparently.

"Sit…sit… Gadhvi saheb!" Chavan gestured towards the chair almost sincerely. Gadhvi was pleasantly surprised at this development. Satan is happy, he thought and took a seat.

"Tell me the whole thing again. From the start. Till today, this very minute. Spare no detail. Go," He spoke in a menacing low baritone that Gadhvi loathed.

For the next 15-20 minutes, Gadhvi laid out every detail. He didn't see the point because everything was already known to Chavan. In fact, he was merely following instructions since the discovery.

The verbatim ended, and Ramesh Chavan was silent for 2 minutes. Gadhvi could feel the inner lining of his stomach burning up.

"Aashish Purie has flown out?"

"Yes, Sir. His flight took off at 12:30 PM."

"Forensics have taken charge of the bungalow? And the hammer?"

"Yes, Sir. The submissions are in our custody here and being analysed as we speak, and the hammer is with the lab. All the reports are expected by EOD today or tomorrow morning." Gadhvi was parroting every answer.

"Hmm…now listen carefully…."Gadhvi hated this part.

"Close the case the moment forensic reports are in. No loose ends. There is no mention of this in the media. That's number one."

"Yes, Sir."

"Have discreet surveillance on Kamble and his child prodigy. My guys will be in touch with your PA and driver."

"Understood, Sir."

"Listen Gadhvi….I don't believe in fate, God and coincidences, but I am a firm believer in destiny. Although plausible, this is all very … what's the word… convenient. It looks like it's done for now. I am digging up everything I can find on Colonel Purie. The only way I will believe all this is if he was present there that night. But I am careful. You be careful, too. Be very, very careful."

"Yes, Sir."

IGP stood up, gave an over-enthusiastic salute and proceeded to the door.

"Gadhvi…" His voice boomed. Gadhvi turned around frantically.

"No matter what happens, no one …… and I mean NO ONE should be on the road to Alibaug. Do you understand?"

"Loud and clear, Sir."

NOVEMBER 11TH, 2023.
Patil Residence, 5:00 PM.

Neel failed to convince the management at St. Matthews orphanage to engage with him on Joel D'Souza. He couldn't tell whether they were inconsiderate, unbothered, unaware or simply uninterested. He rang the bell, and Mrs. Patil greeted him with a warm smile. It was already evening, and Neel was clamouring for Mrs. Patil's adrak chai. He was a coffee nut, and here he was, jonesing for ginger tea. Shiksha would have killed him had she known.

"You sit, Neel; I will get some tea for us." She was not asking, so Neel just smiled.

The living room was tastefully done. The furniture was not exclusive or expensive, but it was just right. It spoke about how simple and graceful Mrs. Patil was. The wall of memories drew his attention. It encapsulated all of their time together as a family. Neel noticed something and made a mental note to ask.

The tea was absolutely divine. He admitted that enjoying this brew was akin to cheating on Shiksha, but what the hell?

"Anything new has come up? I am sure I told you everything, Neel."

"Yes Ma'am…I will just take 5 minutes of your time. I could have done this over the phone, but sometimes talking face-to-face is just ……more fruitful."

She nodded slowly, expressing her agreement or nudging Neel to come to the point.

"Ma'am, last time we spoke, you confirmed how your husband almost changed overnight around the time when the year 2011 started. The newfound money, new life… new healthier habits both physically and spiritually……."

Neel was treading slowly but got encouraged as she finally nodded.

"Also, the money trail was established by RC Kaka. Now it's my fault completely because I missed my obvious follow-up question…… What happened then?"

"What do you mean?" She was puzzled.

"What happened which changed him… any event…. any person….I mean, something big must have happened… right?"

"I don't know Neel….seriously. And I never pried on it because, as I said earlier, it was all for the better, you know."

Neel was deflated a little, but he knew the right answers only came to rightly asked questions. Years and years of reading and practising detection had taught Neel that a correct question is almost always as important as a right answer. He formulated something in his mind and proceeded.

"It is safe to assume that it was around New Year's, but it was much more than… a common resolution, right…. There had to be an antecedent…a trigger for something that…. life-changing and transformative. Maybe something happened on New Year's Eve 2010/11… maybe…" He left the question hanging to jog her memory.

"I wouldn't know Neel because he was not with us on December 31st, 2010…the New Year's Eve."

Bang,….the right question. Bingo!

"Where was he, Ma'am?" Neel's heart rate was elevated now.

"Alibaug… with some colleagues or friends, I don't remember … but some small work trip got extended. I didn't mind because he was paid a decent amount. Those were frugal days, you know…."

"Alibaug!" Neel let out a sigh. Finally, he thought.

There was the clue that had been missing all along. Alibaug and around New Years 2010/2011.

"Thank you so much for your time, Ma'am!"

Neel took her leave and was at the door when he turned around.

He pointed at the wall full of memories. "That's a beautiful time capsule of memories, Ma'am. Believe me, I know its value."

It drew a smile out of Mrs. Patil.

"I mean, you had some good times. I can see Sir being healthier, more fit in later years and even more hair. I mean, did he have a hair transplant or something?"

"No, no….he didn't want the hassle. He just wanted more confidence, so he started wearing a weave…a hairpiece, I mean. A half wig if you will."

Neel bid adieu and raced out because too many things were wide open, and there was too little time. He had a hunch. Something was just not right.

He texted Kamble on his way back.

November 11th, 2023.

Andheri Police Station, 7:00 PM

Kamble was staring at the forensic report. He was expecting it, of course. The murder weapon is a 95% match as per the post-mortem reports of all 5 victims. There was no DNA or evidence of any other kind on the hammer. No fingerprints. He was expecting that, too.

IGP Gadhvi was not in the office the whole day. However, he did call in the early evening and instructed to formally close the case as soon as possible. Absolutely no news to the media.

Kamble meant it when he invoked Occam's razor in the morning at Clarence House. The mountain of evidence pointed at Colonel. But there were 2 problems. Two things were bothering him.

Firstly, why close the case? Why can't the investigation keep going? Why did this all happen? It has not been resolved yet, so why shut it down?

Secondly and more importantly, Paul and PP, Gadhvi's thugs, were in the office all day even though the asshole never turned up. This had never happened. He had a hunch they were there for him. He was being followed and monitored. Quite brazenly, too. This was pissing him off.

He wanted answers, too. But he had to be discreet.

He messaged Neel in person, not in the group.

Let's meet tomorrow at 11:00 AM. Same coffee house.

But right now, he needed something urgently. A good night's sleep.

32
NOVEMBER 11ᵀᴴ, 2023

Neel had to collect his thoughts and organise them. There were 2 theories in his mind - one was obvious, and the other was way too radical. He was torn. His mind was not ready to believe that the obvious theory was correct. His mind didn't agree that the Colonel did it. And his heart was praying to God that the other theory was just a figment of his wild imagination. But he couldn't brush off a certain pattern which he had seen. He couldn't afford to share it with anyone, either. Not as yet. Not till he checked it for himself. While he was checking, he would pray that it was all just a coincidence. A figment of his wild imagination.

Gau and Shiksha were having sandwiches and chai as Neel entered in.

"Hey Neel, you have to taste this sandwich…I mean Shiksha….you….you…" Gau stuffed the last morsel even before he could finish his sentence.

"No thanks," Neel replied curtly. He picked up his laptop and parked himself at the corner of the bed.

"Neel… let the sandwich be…what will you eat …tell me… what do you need?" Shiksha asked politely.

"I need, want, desire, yearn, crave….a drink Shiksha. Because I am stuck, and that's what I need. A stiff drink solves everything."

Gau took the hint. His eyes met Shiksha, and they sat down quietly.

"Sorry guys…"Sighed Neel. "Can we just work, please? I need help."

"Of course," the duo echoed.

Neel got up and started walking like he always did when thinking loud.

"Remember the unanswered questions this morning. I think I had a breakthrough courtesy of Mrs. Patil. The big event. Antecedent to this vendetta. What? When? Where? We have 2 out of those 3. Something happened in Alibaug at the end of the year 2010 or early 2011. Just to be safe, let's have a time window of a month, from December 15th, 2010, to January 15th, 2011. We don't know what happened, but we can dig. Right?"

Neel was looking for support and enthusiasm.

"That narrows down the search a lot. Also, if we can place Colonel Purie there at the right place at the right time, then that ties a neat little bow on top of the theory." Gau was charged.

"Absolutely" Neel reluctantly agreed. "So Gau, now we have a narrow search channel. Go through everything that happened in that one-month period in Alibaug. Anything unsavoury that warranted revenge. Right from a pickpocket arrested to a murder. Anything which involves a loss and creates an aggrieved party."

Gau gave a thumbs-up without even looking up. He put on his headphones and his game face.

"Shiksha…search everything on Colonel again. His history, socials, and his son Aashish, but this time, we have a specific thread. We need to tie him and/or his family to Alibaug."

"Got it. I am on it." Shiksha was ready. "But what will you do, Neel?" she had to ask.

Neel picked up his laptop and went right up to the whiteboard, which was still displayed.

VG.	JA.	RT.	JD.	EP
03/04/11.	16/03/12.	23/06/13.	07/01/19.	19/01/21

Those dates. There was a pattern in those dates. He got to work and mumbled.

"I am going to check something that is bugging me, Shiksha. And just pray that I am wrong."

NOVEMBER 11ᵀᴴ, 2023.
Mumbai, 11:00 PM

Ramesh Chavan allowed himself to relax a little in the jacuzzi of his 4000 sq ft apartment overlooking the city that never sleeps. His team had just informed him of the Colonel's connection with Alibaug. It turned out his wife was born and brought up there. It seems her family was quite influential. After marriage, the family usually spent the holiday season in Alibaug at their palatial family home. Colonel's son moved to the USA in the early nineties, shortly after his wife died. But he kept the routine up. He welcomed every New Year right there in Alibaug. So he must have been there then. He couldn't possibly have witnessed the accident, let alone figure out that it was not an accident. So how, then?

But Colonel was there. That's good. He is dead. Even better. But was he acting alone, or is someone still out there looking for … the accident causes? That thought bothered him.

He thought maybe he was getting paranoid, but he knew damn well that only the paranoid survived. The cemetery is full of the ones who took it easy.

NOVEMBER 11ᵀᴴ, 2023.
Clarence House, 11:30 PM

Unfortunately, Neel found a pattern. It was eerie and did not make sense, but it fits. There was no logic to it, but it fits. It couldn't possibly be true, but it fits. His chain of thought was fortunately broken by a loud noise of YES! YES! YES! Gau was standing up with both his hands raised up in the air like Mohammed Ali. Shiksha was laughing, and Neel was sure the fool had found something.

"Guys…I don't know if we have something right, but we do have a lot of potential candidates. Ok…come close. I will show you all the incidents. I have each one in a separate tab."

Neel and Shiksha were on either side on their knees while Gau was manoeuvring the system.

"There are a total of 21 events of interest where at least one of the parties involved are even slightly dismayed, which took place in Alibaug in the stipulated time and have a digital record."

Gau looked at either of them for effect.

"4 murders, 12 accidents and 5 altercations/misdemeanours. So, we do……."Gau was dramatising a bit much for Neel's taste.

"Leave out the altercations and misdemeanours. We can visit them later if we don't find anything relevant in the other 2 categories, Gau. And, of course, let us start with murders first." Neel sort of laid out the instructions.

"Right." Gau rolled through 4 tabs one by one.

"Property dispute in the extended family, Adultery, politically motivated and unsolved as it is a kind of murder/suicide. You guys go through them, and then we look at the respective paper cuttings."

Gau rolled back and let Neel and Shiksha have a look.

"This politically motivated murder looks interesting. Who is the accused? Is it solved?" Mumbled Neel.

"Bullseye Neel Mantri - The accused name is Vinayak Ghatak, our first victim." Gau stood up and tipped his metaphoric hat. "You are welcome."

"Ha ha ha….Neel, that's not all. I think we got it. Look at this." Shiksha offered her laptop.

"Our Colonel was actually married into Alibaug. His wife was born and brought up there. In fact, she was the sole heiress to quite a fortune and a huge palatial house. Her family was quite influential, and there are tonnes of dated pictures of her before and after marriage. Her father was a successful industrialist, so the local newspaper loved her, it seems."

Shiksha took a pause to switch to a different tab in the browser.

"There are many pictures of the couple with a very young Aashish too. It looks like the family holidayed quite frequently in their palatial house, which she inherited. And look at Aashish's socials, man. If you think he is hot now, look at his pictures from 20 years ago. Rock and roll roadie. Yum!"

Shiksha stood up to stretch, still waiting for Neel, who was lost, to react.

Gau sensed the opportunity and took the stage.

"As per Kaka, the Colonel lost his wife in the early 90s, and Aashish moved to the States. He never remarried and took retirement from military service after Kargil with due honours. So, a widower is in search of some quiet time. And ex-military. It is safe to say he got the house, and it is also safe to say he must have enjoyed and relaxed there at least once a year. And if you add political murder with Vinayak Ghatak involved, this combination looks ripe to substantiate the Colonel being the vigilante." Gau stood on the bed, this time with his Mohammed Ali pose.

Shiksha was laughing and clapping.

"How the fuck does that nonsense substantiate anything....! That's just confirmation bias!" Neel's abnormal decibel levels brought the jubilations to a screeching halt.

"Whoa Neel...I didn't say it substantiated ....I said it was ripe to be substantiated....I mean, a case can be made...... ."Gau became defensive.

"Bullshit....this proves nothing, and nothing is fucking ripe to be substantiated. Fancy words don't mean anything. They are just used to sound smart. That's all."

Gau was speechless for a moment at the escalation.

"Neel....what the fuck......"Gau raised his hand to stop Shiksha from retaliating on his behalf.

"Fancy words to sound smart, huh....of course!!! You are the one who is spewing out fancy words here....Tabula Rasa... Confirmation bias....and whatnot. Basically, there is only one OG in this world. God's gift to mankind - Neel

Mantri, huh!" Gau was sarcastic and wanted Neel to react, but he didn't.

"You know what your problem is, Neel… you live in denial. No… no…you live in a bubble… in a world you created in your head where you are, Sherlock, Elon Musk, Shahrukh Khan, and Shane Warne all fused into one giant bullshit ball…" Gau was frothing now.

"Hey hey … c'mon guys….relax now!" Shiksha immediately tried to douse the fire. But it was too late.

"I live in denial, huh? I live in a bubble. Well…Gau… it's better than living in a closet!"

"Neel Mantri…you shut your mouth this instant," Shiksha shouted at her loudest best and tried to push Neel out of the room. But the shit had already hit the fan.

Gau stood there quietly. His expression changed from anger to surprise to heartbreaking disappointment. He didn't move or say anything for 2 minutes. Neel went out in the open and lit a cigarette. Shiksha remained frozen, not knowing what to say or do.

And slowly, after what felt like an eternity, Gau made a long walk out.

Shiksha tried to stop him.

Shiksha tried to hug him.

Shiksha tried to console him.

But Gau needed to leave that very instant. And he did.

33
NOVEMBER 12ᵀᴴ, 2023

Neel had sent 20 audio messages to Gau up till now. No revert. Neel understood the anger. You get betrayed by the person who is your strongest confidante. But Neel was not sorry for what he said. He was just sorry for what he said and how he said it. He loved Gau, and he wanted his friend to live with freedom. Neel had known all along. It was time. It had been time for quite some time now. Gau needed to be pushed. But not like this. He hurt his friend. Bad Neel Mantri.

Neel was feeling like shit, and a drink could salvage the night. But Shiksha would be mad. Why does he care so much about that? He would lose face in front of her if she got to know him that he definitely cared about her. She didn't turn up after that … scene. She must have slept still mad at him. He wanted to wake her up and explain, but importantly, he needed a drink.

"Care to join me, Neel?" A familiar voice boomed from out in the open, almost scaring Neel.

An amused Neel peered out and found Shiksha holding two half-full glasses of what seemed like dark rum. Neel was smiling ear to ear as he walked and took one. Clink. Cheers.

Gone in one gulp. Neel Mantri was feeling warm and good inside.

"Thank you for that," and he lit one.

"I know you said that you would only drink by raising a toast upon solving this case. But it's okay, Neel……. Don't be so hard on yourself. Things happen in their time. Enjoy. Be gentle to yourself. You owe it to you. I know you want one more. Go get it, tiger!!!"Shiksha took a sip with swag.

Neel rushed to the corner and fixed one.

"Things happen at their time, huh… Shiksha….it was high time….I am his best friend….I mean… when……" A big gulp interrupted the statement.

"Look at you. You really are a narcissistic asshole, Neel, and there is nothing wrong with it. You do love Gau. You want him to live free. But stop justifying what you did. You said what you said purely to get back at him just because your ego was hurt. He is not yours to out. You can't take away his life-changing and life-defining moment from him. It was….his decision. Do you understand that? That's why and where you fucked up." Shiksha was a little loud because she wanted to be.

Neel looked away because he was being shown the mirror. But he was listening.

"If someone loves you, cherish it, relish it, protect it, respect it, and return it if you can reciprocate, BUT NEVER ever do you take it for granted. Capisce asshole?"

Shiksha finished her drink in one big gulp eliciting a smile from Neel. She gave a salute and slowly made her way for the stairs.

"How long have you known, by the way…?"She was curious

"I have known for quite some time. Some observations. Some deductions. I mean…we have watched lots of porn together….he never…"

"Ok… ok…fine… whatever. Good night." She turned around to walk down.

"Shiksha…when did you know….?"

"A woman always knows …….always ……and she knows everything Neel Mantri."

34.
NOVEMBER 12TH, 2023

Clarence House, 9:00 AM

There was excitement in the air in Clarence House. India was playing its last league match against the Netherlands before the semi-final on Wednesday, which meant it was party day. Drinks are at Balli's Bar, followed by mehfil at home. Amma and Ibu were down with their morning walk with an extra spring in their steps. The oldies were having their morning brew curated by Shiksha and were neck-deep in the newspapers.

"Say Shiksha …all well, beta…? The decibel level last night was a little… unusual, let's say…." Amma had to ask.

"All fine … just Gau being Gau… that's all. Now… now… what is the plan for today? What are my favourite boys up to?" Shiksha swiftly steered away.

Ibu finished his chai with a loud slurp, which was exactly the kind she hated. Seeking her attention may be.

"Well…the usual. We are at Balli around 3 and watch men in blue take on the orange army. Our support is laced with beer and finger food, and then we come back home and see India win, where Chef Shiksha will enamour us with her legendary Laal Maans!!!

"Oh my God… look at you….Assumptions galore!!! You already know India will win….and I will make Laal Maans….huh!" Shiksha loved the energy. She picked up the black coffee and headed upstairs.

"Oye Shiksha … Why don't all you guys join us at Ballis…I will call Kamble, too. It's a Sunday!"

"Ok, Amma…"Shiksha was already out.

Neel was still sleeping but not soundly. His usual soft snore was missing, and he woke up as soon as Shiksha entered.

"Coffee… sleepyhead!!!"

Neel checked his phone immediately in case Gau had replied. Nope. Zilch.

"He is still mad *yaar* Shiksha…."Neel got dressed.

"Still… Still mad……It happened last night….almost midnight. Cmon give him time to process your … asshole-ry and jackassery……. Don't worry; he will come around. By the way, weren't you meeting Kaka today?

"Shit…" Neel inhaled his coffee and rushed to the washroom.

November 12ᵀᴴ, 2023.

Coffee House, Andheri Police Station, 10:55 AM.

During the short rickshaw ride to the coffee house from home, Neel had already called Gau thrice and sent him 10 voice messages. It was too much. Shiksha was right. Give him time. But Neel missed him. Well, not exactly. Neel missed knowing that Gau was okay.

As he paid cash to the surprised driver, he could see Kaka was already there. He rushed inside, and right before he sat down, he had a text from Kaka.

Kamble gestured to the waiter for a coffee and nudged Neel to read it right now.

KAKA

I am being brazenly followed, and in all probability, you are too. I deliberately called you here to keep these assholes in sight. It can be turned into an advantage later. But be very, very careful and, needless to say, act normal.

Neel felt the tinge of excitement. Youth does that to you. Being careful was not the first response. It was a distant second after the adrenaline rush.

Neel gave the entire download of yesterday's research. The findings that the search generated - Colonel's Alibaug connection, conversation with Mrs. Patil, and Aashish's socials basically all involved in the obvious theory. He kept his wild discoveries to himself. Yet. It was important not to invite Kaka's wrath right now.

"Hmmm…so you are saying a big trigger is an event in Alibaug towards the year-end 2010."

"Right Kaka…"

"What is it…do you have that research, too?" Kamble was genuinely interested.

Neel took out the printouts of all the cases Gau had searched, which were available in public records and media archives.

Kamble went through all of it on a surface level.

"There are what….almost….21 incidents here….but…"

"Kaka. not everything is in the public domain. If possible, can we get some unpublished information about these cases, and if just one name …one date……anyone…. anything… …..comes up with a name or a date which fits in our current knowing… then… bam!" Neel was careful not to raise his voice.

"What is it you are not telling me, Neel?"

Neel was taken aback but regained composure, which was in vain now because Kaka had exposed him.

"There is an alternate theory… a wildfire theory which is there. I sensed a pattern which exists but doesn't make any sense as of now, so….I will not say till I am sure, Kaka. It could be distracting…"

"Good. That's mature. Let it brew, but don't spit it out sooner. You are learning. Ok… let me get these cases checked. I currently have a junior officer posted in Alibaug. I have to assume that whatever it is must be protected and watched. So it has to be hush-hush… Chal, see you around 4." Kamble got up.

"4…today….where…why…?"

"Oh, you don't know…Amma called up. We are all meeting at Balli's Bar after lunch. India is playing today. And God knows I can use a chilled one. Chal. Bye."

"Umm…Kaka. One more thing." Kamble saw the seriousness on Neel's face, so he sat down again.

"Mrs. Patil also said her husband used to wear a hairpiece and a half wig of sorts. There is no mention of that in the findings list. It may be important, maybe not. But can we check or better…trace?"

Kamble liked it. Attention to detail. He nodded in affirmation, wore his shades and walked out. The goons watching made no effort to conceal themselves and followed him.

Neel made one more call to Gau before leaving. The number was switched off.

35
November 12ᵀᴴ, 2023

Simplicity mixed with utter purity will always have its own swag. Why do true cricket fans still clamour for a riveting test series? Dressed in pearly whites, lush green grass, and red cherry, just look at the colour pallet. And there was even a contest between bat and ball. I can bowl however I want; you bat however you want. Let's see who wins. Wow. It's such a cliché when the oldies say it was amazing in our times. The young ones are not at fault. They have not seen it. They may be unlucky but not at fault. That's why Neel lived in the past; it was just better. And the beautiful wall of cricket and rock-n-roll history Asif had created in his bar, an old soul like Neel could just stand for hours and admire.

Sir Viv Richards, Dennis Lillie, Sunil Gavaskar, Rolling Stones, Pink Floyd, Sachin Tendulkar, Brian Lara and Shane Warne. Wow. Neel could just stand there and wonder and he would have if not for Asif.

"Say, Sherlock… you are early. You even beat me and Dad. Long time chief!"

Effortless swag Asif exuded. The man's man. And he always smelled amazing. This is what Neel always thought whenever he hugged Asif, and today, it was no different.

"I came straight from…uh…somewhere. The gang will be here soon, I suppose. Let me meet Balraams uncle and come back."

Asif nodded as he made his way to the kitchen with an over pleasing manager explaining him today's specials.

Balraam Pandit, loaded with money and age-defying muscles, was on his throne behind the counter. Neel touched his feet and was blessed with a pat on the head. A gentle pat with that strong Hulk hand also felt hard. Not a hit, but hard enough. Balli will never hurt him. He was not that careless. It's just he was that strong.

Neel must have met Balli hardly 20 times in his 21 years on this planet. He was around a lot when Neel lost his mother, but he hardly spoke. Hell, not even Amma and Ibu can claim to have spoken a lot with Pandit Ji, and they knew each other for more than half a century.

"Kya Neel…how's the detective agency going? Amma had mentioned it some time back. Good. Good. Do what you want to do. Never mistake education for academics. And don't forget to get rich."

Balli did not wait for any replies. No small talk. He buried his face in the screen immediately.

Here is a man, Neel thought. Big. Burly. Rich. Womaniser. But above all, wise.

"We are batting first …here…you are 21 naa …? Not that its important." Asif offered a beer.

"Yes, Sir. Cheers" Neel reminded himself to drink slowly as he clinked the pints and had his first sip.

"The apple doesn't fall far from the tree… huh, Neel!" Commented Amma as the whole gang roared with laughter. Amma, Ibu and Shiksha walked in. Everyone acknowledged

Balli first with a salute or head nod and returned an acknowledgement.

Asif greeted the oldies and patted Shiksha's head, who was giggling like a schoolgirl at this touch. She had a massive crush on Asif since time immemorial, and Neel didn't blame her. Good taste in men, he thought. Their VIP table with the best view and ventilation was ready. Asif gestured to the waiter for drinks.

"Get one more usual, Asif; Kamble is reaching in 2 minutes."

Kamble walked in and, after pleasantries with the host, eyed Neel's beer a little bit longer. But gave a wry smile and settled with the group as Indian batting unsettled the Dutch bowling attack.

Indian batting was on song. Legendary fish fingers and seek kebabs were being washed down with flowing beer amongst loud cheers.

Asif was sneaking a smoke in the corner next to the wall of honour with cricketers and rockstars plastered all over. There were also pictures of Asif in his 20s being a roadie. He was there with GnR, Pearl Jam and Metallica, to name a few. Shiksha and Neel excused themselves from the group in the hope of a sneaky drag.

"Look at that Shiksha - That's what you call class. What life have you lived, Asif? Respect."

Shiksha went closer and shrieked "Woooooow"… a bit too loud.

"Look at you, Asif. Long hair. With ears and nose pierced. And the all-leather look. Woooow." Chucked Shiksha, hitting Neel with a whip of jealousy.

Neel looked closely. It was indeed Asif.

"Fuck, man. I didn't notice. I thought it was one of the band members. Asif…you really looked like a rockstar. I mean, you still do…but back then….I mean wow…"

Neel was pushed aside before he could finish as Shiksha was busy taking pictures.

"C'mon guys….I am flattered and a bit embarrassed, too." Asif left as he saw the manager requesting his presence in the kitchen.

Shiksha was looking at the wall and clicking pictures while Neel was looking at her. Shiksha was milking the moment. She amplified her admiration to amplify the jealousy Neel Mantri was feeling. But it was enough she thought.

"I spoke to Gau."

"When…? I have been trying since…"

"He has gone to Pune to visit his grandma. He came out Neel. To his family. His parents and elder sister. They were shocked and didn't handle it well. So, to give them time and, more importantly, to give himself time…he left for a few days. Understandable. Right."

Neel didn't know what to say. He missed Gau. He felt helpless.

"Is he okay?"

Shiksha smiled at this vulnerability and helplessness because it was authentic. She caressed his cheek.

"No, but he assured me he would be. It had to happen someday. Don't worry. Chal, let's go home."

"Home? Everyone is here, but…"

"Ya… for now. These oldies want to have Laal Maans tonight, and it takes a minimum of 3 hours to prepare. And more importantly, I will not cook alone, so come with me and keep me entertained while I slog for these shameless carnivores. Any problem?"

Neel smiled. "No, Ma'am."

They were about to leave when Shiksha stopped short and stared at one of the pictures at the top left corner. She was sure she had seen it somewhere. In fact, recently. She couldn't place it where exactly, and she was in a rush. She quickly zoomed in. Click.

36
NOVEMBER 12TH, 2023

Mumbai, 8:00 PM

She came with her younger brother to Mumbai to escape poverty. But poverty followed them. And like how. Her retired father, with peanuts for pension, couldn't fight an aggressively spreading cancer in her mother's breasts. The breasts which nourished her. Nurtured her. The cancer was aggressive, and expensive chemotherapy presented a chance. There are no guarantees, but there is a chance. And she was determined to give her mother that chance. It's only the poor who get sick. She didn't believe it at first, but whenever she visited the government hospital in her village or, for that matter, in Mumbai, she was convinced that the poor had a copyright on misery.

She had graduated with honours, and her younger brother had stood first in the district in his class XII exams. He wanted a year off to prepare for the medical entrance exam. He wanted to become a doctor so that he could save his mother. She vowed to preserve and nurture this rare combination of brilliance of mind, innocence in heart, and steely resolve in intent.

She sold all her jewellery and all her savings from tuition classes she had been taking for the past 8 years, amounting to a paltry sum of 2 lakh rupees. She handed half to her father to keep her mother alive, took the other half and her sibling, and came to Mumbai, the city of dreams, the city of hope for her.

She was left with 500 rupees on her second day in Mumbai after she paid security and 3 months" rent for the cheapest lodgings in a slum, a month's ration and utilities and 20% fees of the coaching institute she enrolled her brother in. She was happy but. It was all an investment. She immediately got a job in a local beauty parlour to keep the household running. She picked up two-morning jobs as a housemaid before her parlour job started and 2 after. Fifteen hours of work a day. But her take home would be 5 times her father's pension. She smiled at the positive imbalance. One day at a time.

But poverty, which followed them, adulterated the teenage mind of her brother, who fell in bad company. She didn't even know he skipped classes, did drugs and got involved in peddling and a local betting syndicate. How would she know? She barely had time to sleep, let alone keep tabs on her brother.

And then, one day, the police came knocking. The syndicate with deep pockets went scot-free, but they needed a scapegoat for the token arrest the cops were going to make. And her brother was the perfect target. They came. They saw. They conquered. They found a small amount of weed and tuned mathematics on her brother. The charge was intended to sell. Her entire world came crashing down. She pleaded, begged, cried, howled, but no one listened. She forced herself into the chambers of **Bada Sahab** to beg for clemency. He saw her, and before the constables could hurl her away, he intervened. He listened. He heard her out. The whole thing. Her situation. Her family's situation. She saw a trickle of hope somewhere. He told her to come back the next day.

The next day, **Bada Sahab** was sitting with the public prosecutor. In front of her, he instructed the public defender to make a strong case for the boy. He then called his subordinate to ensure the boy was not roughed up in jail. She touched his feet. He gave her his personal number and promised to follow-up religiously. He even took her number, just in case. He came like a white knight in her life. Like a fairy tale.

But life is not a fairy tale. There is no fairy. There is no Narnia. There is no Santa Claus. There is no angel. There is no heaven. But there is hell. And it's right here on Earth. In every city, especially in Mumbai.

After 2 days, she got a call from him. He wanted to meet at the lawyer's house to discuss her testimony. But when she reached, there was no lawyer but just him in a robe having a drink. A woman always knows. It took her 10 seconds to understand what had happened, what was happening and what was going to happen. Feeble father, Dying Mom and imprisoned brother. She didn't have a choice. So, in a split second, she put a dagger into her dreams and closed the door behind her. He didn't have to say anything because she didn't want to listen. She didn't want to hear any more white lies. More importantly, she didn't want to hear his voice. But she had to.

She had to hear his incoherent mumblings as he defiled her. She had to hear how pretty and tight she was. She had to hear that she was too skinny and that she could put on some weight, especially on her ass and thighs. She had to hear her hopes and her dreams crash and burn on the ground. She had to hear that he liked it when she called him Bada Sahab and insisted that she keep repeating it when he was on top of her.

She finally had to hear that she was going to live in this house from now on and he would keep visiting. She had to hear that from now on she is his mistress. Or **goomah** as the Italian mob bosses called them as he had heard it somewhere.

She was quiet. All this while. What could she have said?

"Your brother is in thick soup but believe me I will keep trying. Don't worry. Ok. This house has everything you need. The rent is paid. The kitchen is working. I will keep giving you monthly stipend to stock up food and utilities. And also my favourite brand of alcohol and cigarettes."

He was getting dressed as he was talking. The sound of his zipper haunted her till date. It was like an audio nail in the coffin. Monthly stipend. Money. She can at least send some home to her ailing mother.

"Can I go to work, please? I need to send money back home."

"Of course. Of course. What else will you do here all day? I might come to see you 3 times a month. Nice little arrangement for you, isn't it." And then he smiled. He kissed her, and he smiled. Arrangement. Just like every girl dreams of. Arrangement. She wanted to kill him there and then. But she didn't. It was she who died instead. Inside.

She decided to put up with it till her brother was out. It had been more than year now. Every time she asked him about her brother she was met with fake assurances the first 3 times and a tight slap the last couple of times.

She didn't know what to do until they showed up.

Once bitten, twice shy.

She was terrified at first how they knew everything about him and her situation. They had kind eyes. She could see they meant well. She had a feeling they hated him as much as she did. They ensured her mother got the chemotherapy just last month and promised to take care of her brother's case. In return, they wanted him. Defenceless. Alone. Unaware. They wanted to eliminate him. It was overdue. But not a word to anyone, they said. She obliged gladly. She just got a call from one of them. He wanted to know if **Bada Sahab** was coming anytime next week. The call was a bit too late because he was in the shower here. She wished they had called yesterday.

But she wanted to extract his next visit from him. He never shared in advance. He would just turn up like today.

"My towel!" he almost shouted.

She broke her chain of thought and almost ran with the towel.

The devil came out drying himself. She had his drink ready. And his cigarettes.

He was kind of happy today. And he had visited after almost a month. More than a month actually. This had never happened before. He looked like he came out of a storm. Alive. He looked relieved. She didn't like it. She wanted him miserable.

His phone rang.

"Paul... what is it?"

"Hmm...hmm... when?....and then... ok."

He turned his back towards her and continued in a soft voice. But she heard.

"Not a moment out of sight. Do it in shifts if you have to. Oh yes, they will. Just tell them it is IGP Deven Gadhvi's order. I want 24/7 eyes on Kamble. And if you screw this up, Paul, then you see...."

He was sullen again. Good.

"My wife and kids are going out on Tuesday morning on 14th of November for couple of days. I will spend the 14th night here. Cancel whatever you have …. Understood?"

She nodded fervently in affirmation. And he left.

She typed the message literally the moment he was out of the door.

He would be spending the Tuesday night here. November 14th.

NOVEMBER 12TH, 2023.
Mumbai, 10:00 PM

Ramesh Chavan was not happy. He got multiple calls from his sources at the police station. Gadhvi was not the only cockroach on his payroll. Kamble was meeting that boy. Strike one. Kamble was fiddling with old case files in the evidence room. Strike 2. And the source overheard him talking to a junior cop in Alibaug. Strike fucking 3. He called up a number.

"Hello Jadhav….how is it going?"

"Chavan Saheb! My good fortune you called. Tell me Sir how can I be of service!"

"Ha ha… nothing urgent right now. I was just wondering would you want to contest the assembly elections early next year ….Are you ready and prepared?"

"Sir…Sir…me…Sir…absolutely Sir. I will be honoured. Thank you so…."

"Yeah…yeah…ok….But are you sure you have a strong hold over the Alibaug junta?"

"Sir…try me. I control Alibaug. I run it. I mean, I run it on your behalf, Sir. Trust me."

"Good to know, Jadhav." For the next 10 minutes, Chavan gave a "need to know" version of events. And a detailed set of instructions.

"Understood Bhau…you rest assured. Nothing happens in Alibaug that I don't get to know about."

Chavan was getting tired of this pompous loud mouth.

"Also, Jadhav, do you have someone who can take care of things in a special and untraceable way if need be…… are you getting me?"

Of course, Jadhav was getting it. That was his bread and butter before white kurta pyjama took over.

"Just say the word, Bhau….it will happen, and it will be 100% untraceable. My word."

"I will be in touch."

Chavan didn't like people who talked big, but on short notice, this loudmouth could serve the purpose. Also, that idiot *Chamdi* Gadhvi couldn't be trusted.

37

NOVEMBER 12ᵗʰ, 2023

Clarence House, 10:30 PM.

This victory would make India's World Cup campaign 9/9 so far, and the noise in Clarence House was evidence of it. The whole gang was back at the house for Laal Maans. And there was a new addition today, Asif. Everyone sat in the seating area on the terrace. But the cook inside Asif followed the aroma and went straight to the kitchen. He was walking with semi-closed eyes, breathing in the aroma and waltzing his way over to the kitchen, almost colliding with Neel, who was carrying drinks for everybody.

"Shiksha…Shiksha…my special child. What is this fragrance? How dare you make something that smells so …….heavenly? God bless!!!"

Shiksha was beaming with pride. It was kind of being praised by a teacher you had a crush on.

"Awwww…Asif. Thank you. You really wanna know…?"

"Yes, yes,…a thousand times yes."

"Ok….two things. First, the mutton was tenderly cooked on a low to medium flame for the last 2 hours. Slowly releasing its flavours. No pressure cooker. And second…. that earthy zing you smell, that is Rajasthani dum……let me show you!"

Shiksha took the lid off the container, which had mutton curry in it.

"Look at that steel bowl. It had ghee, burning coal and cloves in it. It was partially submerged in the curry and left for 5……." Shiksha suddenly stopped talking as she was hit by a memory bomb. She rushed out of the kitchen, leaving Asif, who was waiting for the whole explanation.

"Ok, got it… that's amazing, year. I can't wait to taste it. Laal Maas!!!!" shouted Asif from behind.

Shiksha rushed to the sitting area, grabbed Neel, and took him into his bedroom.

She took out the picture she had clicked while leaving Balli's Bar and fired Neel's laptop open.

She showed the picture of Asif in a ponytail and leather ensemble, the one with 90s rock Gods Guns n Roses. The original one. The one with Axel and Slash together.

"Look closely, Neel…"

"I know that's Asif Baba. I get he was gorgeous. He is still gorgeous. He is dreamy… blah…blah…blah…."

"Shut up, Neel. Look at the other people in the picture."

"That's Guns n Roses yaar Shiksha."

"Idiot…who is the last guy on the left?"

Neel blew up the picture and focused on the last guy on the left.

"Wait….is it….

"Yes. That is Aashish Purie."

Shiksha went out and gestured for a tipsy Kamble to come into the bedroom. Reluctantly, he picked up his drink and stumbled across the multiple pairs of legs en route to Neel's room. Kamble was feeling light and happy. Breezy, if you will. And the duo peed on his party parade.

Kamble looked at the picture closely for 30 seconds straight.

"Are you sure that's Aashish?"

"Yes Kaka, look the same photograph is in Aashish's social media account too. Of course, it is him."

"Then why didn't Asif tell me…?"

"Tell you what and why, Kaka. The entire thing is known to a few people. We didn't ask. The theory about Colonel Purie and the discovery of that basement is not public knowledge. So maybe he is not aware… you know."

Kamble was completely alert now.

"But they know each other. Aashish came back to India on a sombre occasion after so many years. They didn't meet…?" Kamble was in cop mode now.

"But Kaka… there is no recent picture of them together. This picture is almost 30 years old, so a big leap there… But why don't we ask Asif without … you know …giving it away."

It was dead silence. Everyone was just busy eating. The only noises were of happy drunk people savouring the food. But once a cop, always a cop. Kamble blurted it out.

"Asif…do you know any Aashish Purie?"

Asif had his mouthful. He kept on relishing that morsel and thinking, may be trying to recall and finally nodded his head in affirmation.

"He was my neighbour in Alibaug. I mean, he didn't live there. He often visited in holidays. His grandfather was our neighbour, actually. Wow…such a blast from the past. Why… Kamble?"

"Aashish Purie….arey wo Colonel Purie ka beta?" Said Amma, taking Kamble and Neel aback.

"How do you know him, Amma?" Neel had zero interest in eating now.

"Arey…as Asif said. His father-in-law was Pundit's neighbour, so we have met many times. Drinks like an Irishman, huh? These military folks, I tell you……." Amma kept on eating and didn't bother to finish that sentence.

"But why the Puries…all of a sudden…?" asked Amma and Asif almost together.

Kamble and Neel shared a glance.

"Nothing important….something came up. Will tell you later." Kamble killed it.

And India was officially in semifinal of World Cup 2023 with unblemished track record. They played New Zealand on Wednesday the 15th of November.

38

NOVEMBER 13ᵀᴴ, 2023

Mumbai, 10:30 AM

Kamble stepped out of his house and scanned his neighbourhood. There were no familiar looking people around but the black SUV was definitely familiar. It was safe to assume it was them. If not the SUV then something else but they were around. Kamble was nursing a happy hangover which meant that the head was just a little heavy. Nothing what a hot cup of chai won't fix. But the memories of a great relaxing night followed by a great meal outweighed the heavy head. Happy hangover.

Though it was a Monday morning it was going easy at the police station. Gadhvi was not coming to the office for the whole week though his goons didn't miss a beat to shadow Kamble. So, it was time to enjoy the **adrak chai** with love and patience. Slurp by slurp. Indian style. Kamble was happy in that moment.

And he was right. The ginger tea had worked its charm. Happy hangover to just happy.

Neel's last request had found Kamble making calls to understand the procedure followed in such cases. It involved a drive to the police storage for evidence retention in South Bombay. Well, normally, it would irk him, and he would grudgingly do it, growling with frustration all the time. But not today. Also, it was important for the goons outside not to know where he was going. The teenager inside him chuckled at the prospect of what he was about to do.

An unfit teenager wearing beige shorts, a fluorescent green vest and an unbuttoned white shirt came out of the building. The look was completed with a backpack, shades and a NY baseball cap.

There was a strut in his walk. He was built like a middle-aged man, but the walk was young. Full of possibilities. He slowly jogged out and sat in the auto-rickshaw right outside the building. The goons waiting a little bit outside checked the passenger leaving and were busy talking to each other again. And just like that, Kamble was away for a day of Mumbai tour.

Kamble insisted the driver take it from the inroads and not the highway. It was a chance to explore the melting pot of culture, i.e., Bandra. Imagine this - the posh, exorbitantly priced buildings mostly owned by Bollywood biggies and other Richie riches in one corner and graffiti-laden, chapel-studded, old-school bungalows inhabited by the catholic community in the other. And sprinkle here and there the spirited youth sitting in cosy cafes typing their way to achieving their dreams. What a beautiful and vibrant cocktail.

The auto-rickshaw ride had to end as soon as Bandra ended, as that was the city limit for them. From there, Kamble boarded a black and yellow Fiat taxi, the **kaali peeli.** The Bandra-Worli sea link was a relatively new infrastructure but soon became the backbone of Mumbai. It was the bridge, the connection between new adolescents and budget Mumbai with the old, loaded and a bit snooty Mumbai. Although nothing was linear in Mumbai except its geography may be. So, it couldn't be painted with one brush. But as one climbed down the sea link, the opulence offered by the seafaring apartments of Worli could make anybody feel that one is in August surroundings now. And then comes the Peddar Road leading up to Hughes Road, an avenue for the real kings of South Bombay - the Zoroastrians, the Parsees, the **Bawas,** if you will. It was debatable whether the term **Bawa** was derogatory or not, but what was beyond doubt established truth is that the Parsi community quite literally owned South Bombay or SoBo.

This experience elicited a very cliché response out of Kamble. He was falling in love with Mumbai all over again. It happens. One can try. His taxi turned the final corner. He would have to cross the iconic Café Leopold and Café Mondegar as the government building was at the end of the street. The iconic cafes attracted almost every tourist who visited Mumbai including the terrorist from Pakistan in November 2008. But they were still standing strong, serving a bit of Mumbai in every plate, which was heartily gobbled up by Mumbaikars and tourists alike. There was no mystery where Kamble Saheb was going to have his lunch.

Even your typically dusty government building had a special swag and character if it happens to be in South Bombay. And Police Storage and Evidence Retention was no different although the same could not be said about the staff. The clerical staff behaviour and mannerisms transcends across nation boundaries. It was exactly the same everywhere. Bored. Uninterested. Caustic. And one eye perpetually on the clock.

Kamble introduced himself to the clerk, his designation and his intention both. Without a word or even eye contact the clerk placed a form on the counter. Everything else was rudimentary but the details of evidence being retained was of paramount importance. Kamble double checked everything. The case number was checked twice as that being the primary checkable identity.

Victim Name - Eknath Patil

Date - January 21st, 2021

Evidence - A half wig or a hairpiece used to cover half the skull was worn by the victim. It needs to be retained for further DNA examination in light of some new evidence.

Kamble produced a letter of approval from his superior and attached it. Signed and sealed by IGP Deven Gadhvi. He was absolutely sure it will never be cross checked.

The clerk checked the details and frowned, may be annoyed that why this overweight cop dressed like a man child got everything right in the first attempt. Accuracy is annoying. Bam. Bam. Bam.

The sound of government approval on every document. And lastly the remark. We will send the item to Andheri Police Station as soon as we retrieve it.

That was definitely a problem.

"Umm…Sir. Please don't mail it. Can I be called as soon as it is retrieved? I will come pick it up personally. That way, the time in transit can be saved." The clerk smiled and nodded and loudly banged the form on the counter with a pen. Write it down, he meant. They all think they can get the formality done without their help. But no. The clerk is the last line of defence. The smiling clerk accepted the form and gave the receipt back.

November 13th, 2023.
Clarence House, 2:30 PM

The household had a late and lethargic morning, given the festivities last night. Shiksha reluctantly went to college. And everyone was in the middle of a very long siesta.

Since the ball was now in Kamble's court all Neel Mantri could do was wait and may be process his wild theory. Kaka was yet to get any updates about the 2010/11 cases in Alibaug and whether he traced the wig of Eknath Patil.

But last night had given Neel a sinking feeling. Asif knows Aashish Purie. It was certainly possible and coincidental, but suddenly, this discovery took Neel's theory down a notch on a wildness scale. He had the whole house to himself. The oldies were nursing the aftereffects of a rough night. So he took out his notes and drew the whiteboard closer, which still read.

VG.	JA.	RT.	JD.	EP
03/04/11.	16/03/12.	23/06/13.	07/01/19.	19/01/21

Neel zoned in on the latest victims first. Eknath Patil and Joel D'Souza. Their murder dates were the ones which prompted this germ of an idea in his brain.

JOEL D"SOUZA.	**EKNATH PATIL**
Jan 7th, 2019.	**Jan 19th, 2021**

He knew he had seen these dates. Not in isolation. Together actually. And he had celebrated these dates.

January 19th, 2021, was the day a bruised, battered third-tier Indian Team won the last test match of the India-Australia test series in Gabba, Brisbane. As Rishabh Pant drilled a tired full toss from Josh Hazelwood down the ground for a boundary, the whole nation erupted in joy. Quarantined India was ecstatic that day. It was a historic win as the Aussie fortress of Gabba was broken through. That's why the date was special. It was a historic win, but not the first one. India also won the last tour of 2019, and that was the first on Australian soil.

The first ever series victory was sealed on **January 7th, 2019.** These dates were being flashed together in the news and that's why these twin dates were etched in Neel's memory.

The 2 murder dates were bang on the dates of 2 most important victories of Indian Cricket in the recent past. Now, this could very well be a coincidence had Gau not voiced his observation the other day.

April 2nd, 2011, is the night India won the World Cup 2011. The presentation and the festivities actually and deservedly crept into April 3rd.

April 3rd, 2011 - The murder date of the first victim.

That's why Neel was disturbed. A wild theory germinated in his mind there and then and a simple search further fired it up.

March 16th, 2012 - Master blaster Sachin Tendulkar scored his 100th century.

June 23rd, 2013 - India won the Champions Trophy.

Neel finished the chart, and now it looked like

VG.	JA.	RT.	JD.	EP
03/04/11.	16/03/12.	23/06/13.	07/01/19.	19/01/21
India wins. WC.	Sachin scores. 100th century.	India wins the Champions Trophy	India wins the Test. series vs Aus.	Depleted India Wins vs Aus

Each murder date coincided with a historic achievement for the Indian Men's cricket team. This was not a coincidence for him. But the story didn't end there.

The big gap of 6 years between 2013 and 2019 was rightfully explained by Shiksha. Col. Purie was diagnosed with cancer in 2014, and hence, the initial shock, the second and third opinions on diagnosis, the inevitable chemotherapy and the convalescence explained this gap. It made sense.

But if one looked at Indian Cricket History, which Neel knew at the back of his hand, there were no notable achievements by the team in that period. The team did well, but there was no achievement. No titles are worthy of…iconic celebration. This spooked Neel. Why was this theory wild? It also made sense that while Indian Cricket was growing leaps and bounds and a force to reckon with, there was no notable tangible achievement from 2013 to 2019. It was fitting. Hence the gap. Was it all just a figment of his overactive imagination? He will certainly be perceived as crazy. It seemed that what Neel was saying was that there was somebody who was offering people on the day of a memorable Indian victory like a celebration.

Neel was even surprised at the sound of it. How could he have shared that with Kaka? It doesn't make any sense. Yet.

39

November 13ᵀᴴ, 2023

Andheri, Mumbai, 7:00 PM.

A beautiful day had finally come to an end. Kamble ensured that the rickshaw went right to the doorstep of his building lobby. He saw the black SUV still brazenly parked at the same spot, along with the idiots sitting in it. The man-child got out of the rickshaw and strutted into the lobby undetected. Rashmi Kamble was not home when he left, but now she was. As soon she opened the door and recognised, she burst into a huge laughter. That was going to last for a while. Kamble ran into the bedroom to quickly change and abort the humiliation.

"Oh my God… Why?" Rashmi threw an obvious one.

"What, why….undercover work, obviously."

Kamble had no intention of mentioning the surveillance and the idiots sitting outside as yet. This would have unnecessarily spooked the family.

Kamble got a call from a landline. It was from the Police Evidence Room. The wig was retrieved and was ready for the picking. Kamble thanked the informer and promised to pick it up at 10:30 in the morning.

A shamelessly snickering Rashmi and a blushing Kamble had their dinner discussing the day. His undercover work popped up but was set aside as premature and confidential. The duo then went for a night stroll. He wanted to register his attendance in front of the surveillance party to feign normalcy. And he was successful for now.

Kamble was surfing TV when the phone rang. It was the junior officer from Alibaug who was responsible for digging those old cases. Kamble muted the TV and went into the kitchen.

"Hello, Kamble saheb… this is Mhatre here. Sorry to disturb you so late."

"Arey nahi Mhatre, tell me…."

"Sir, I dug up all the 21 cases. The murders were a dead end, and so were the property dispute altercations. One of the accidents somehow was a little iffy. It was a house fire because of a faulty stove. Mother and 2 kids died in the fire on the spot. And an ailing grandfather who was sleeping outside succumbed to injuries 6 hours later…" Mhatre stopped for an instant.

"What is so iffy about that Mhatre….I mean stove blast incidents are quite common in small towns right,,?"

"Yes, Sir, definitely. It's just that there was no forensic corroboration of the theory. It was just declared the very next day and the file was closed and done…"

This got Kamble thinking for sure. This was not by the book. And early foreclosure of the case… was definitely fishy. Nice catch. Good work Mhatre, Kamble thought.

"That's good observation Mhatre…who was the case officer?"

"The file says Sub-Inspector Deven Gadhvi."

It was as if someone had splashed cold water on his face in freezing winters. His face went white for a second. He had to take a deep breath to calm his heart, which was now beating out of his chest.

"Sir…Sir…are you there?"

"Yes, yes. I am here Mhatre….good work….I…." He was interrupted by an overeager junior cop.

"Sir… it's the same Gadhvi…your boss IGP Gadhvi… I was told he is a big deal now and a success story which came out of Alibaug…"

It was Kamble's turn to interrupt.

"Mhatre…Mhatre….did you say ….you were told….you were told by whom… Did you share this information with anybody else….?"

"I mean yes Sir… only with my immediate boss. That's all. No-one else. I swear."

Kamble knew that if IGP"s name is involved the gossip will cross borders and transmit everywhere. He could only pray that the inevitable happens slower than what he was planning in his head.

"Ok, Mhatre….no problem. One…thank you for your help. Two…I need one last thing…I am coming to Alibaug tomorrow. Can you please pick me up from the jetty port and drive me around a little bit?"

"Absolutely Kamble saheb. I would be honoured…"

"Mhatre….not a word of this to anyone. Please."

Kamble fished out his phone and typed a personal message to Neel.

Wig found. We are going to Alibaug tomorrow noon. Will be back by dinner. Meet me at jetty port near Gateway at 11:45 AM.

40

November 14th, 2023

Clarence House, 8:30 AM

Shiksha entered Neel's room with steaming coffee and found Neel all ready and stuffing a backpack with a long torch, his laptop and power backup, his notes and, oddly, a pair of binoculars.

"Ok….too early for questioning Neel…out with it please."

Neel was a little startled but decided in a split second that there was no point in being discreet with Shiksha. He let her in with everything on the whiteboard. His pattern with murder dates and not believing in Colonel Purie theory in its entirety. Also, Asif knowing Aashish Purie was not sitting well with him as just a coincidence. Shiksha placed the coffee mug and held Neel by his forearms and sat him down.

"Neel…my child…I get it. Ok…All you said right now is incredible but……you know….pointless. And also….also… why are you packing…and that too a binoculars for crying out loud." She sounded worried.

"You have to promise me you will keep this to yourself."

"I won't. Absolutely not. You are off to do something stupid. You tell me right now. Unconditionally. No promises. Or I am calling everyone. Ammmaaaaa……."

Neel stifled her with his hand, pleading her to be quiet.

"Ok. Ok. Fine……….The thing is that Kaka and I are going to Alibaug for a day trip. He found that one of the cases had a direct link. He will fill me in on details when we are en route. Ok. Now, please keep it to yourself. Don't unnecessarily get the oldies worried. I will be back by dinner. Plus, I am not alone. Kaka is with me, you know."

Shiksha kept staring at him. A little more. And then some more. Neel held her gaze all this while.

"Ok…be careful, and if you are not here by dinner, I will tell Amma. Deal?"

"Deal" A relieved Neel shook her hand.

"And what's up with binoculars….you idiot. It happens in movies drama Queen. Might as well keep a pistol too…. ha ha ha…"

She was already outside the room as she finished the sentence, not waiting for his retort. It was good as he didn't have one and was just standing there embarrassed.

November 14th, 2023
Gadhvi Residence, 9:30 AM.

IGP Gadhvi could not wait for his family to go away. Not that anybody in his house could stop him from doing as he pleased, but spending the night with her had never happened. He was getting excited just by the thought of it. He had already planned to leave the office by 4:30-5 and reach her place before 6, beating the traffic. And then there was a single-point agenda. That reminded him to take reinforcements from the pharmacy on his way to the office. He had already received the update that Kamble was at home the whole day yesterday and was planning to take a sick day even today. Good riddance. He didn't want the stress. He instructed his driver, Paul, to ensure that the surveillance was still there outside Kamble's house.

His wife was almost packed, and he couldn't wait to drop her to the airport.

"Come soon now….I will drop you guys to the airport and will go office from there." He announced as he took his wallet, bag and car keys.

"Why… ask Paul to do that, naa! I still need 15 more minutes. Don't rush me!" thundered his wife.

"Paul is on leave, so I am on my own….so you take your time. I will wait…."

Gadhvi sat down and he needed to as he was feeling a little lightheaded. It was because there was not enough blood in the head. The supply was heading down south.

NOVEMBER 14TH, 2023
Kamble Residence, 10:00 AM.

The wannabe middle-aged guy dressed like a man-child kissed his giggling wife good bye and sneaked out of the building with shades and NY baseball cap on. The strut in the walk was back as he jogged away passing the black SUV and hailed an auto-rickshaw. These hired goons were absolutely useless, he almost felt bad for the guy who hired them. Gadhvi? Chavan?

The rickshaw ride was bumpy as usual and ended at Bandra as usual. Kamble slipped into a ***kaali peeli.*** This was going to be a longer ride and a relatively concealed one. Kamble took out the change from his backpack and underwent the makeover, so to speak. The driver was snickering, but it was important for him to at least look like an adult if not a cop.

He had already spoken to Neel. The wig of Eknath Patil needed one more forensic test as per Neel Mantri and it was to be checked for traces of a very specific thing. Kamble was actually quite surprised at that request, as he didn't even remotely see a connection. But he trusted the boy's instincts. And he had been mature about everything.

The same building. The same clerk. The same mind numbingly boring expression. Kamble got directed to room no. 7 on the second floor to collect the evidence. After 2 flights of stairs he was holding a sealed ziplock bag which contained a blood stained wig used by Eknath Patil.

The clock just turned 11. He was right on time.

Twenty minutes later, he was standing in the forensic lab of Mumbai Police. He was quite good friends with the coordinator, so the whole hush-hush thing could play out well. Kamble, anyway, asked for initial discretion, which was not uncommon.

The expert saw the request on the form and frowned.

"I know chief….but I am not mistaken. I want the wig to be tested for those traces only. You can bill me personally for any and all samples you procure for the test."

"Ok, Kamble. You got it. Let me call you as soon as I am done with it."

Kamble grabbed a cab. After a small drive of 10 minutes he reached the jetty port for Alibaug where an excited Neel Mantri was waiting for him.

At precise 12 noon, the sleuth duo was aboard the jetty which started the 1 hour journey to Mandwa. For the first 15 minutes they were mesmerised by the beauty offered by endless ocean and the receding coastline of this beautiful enigma called Mumbai. Then Kamble filled Neel with the accident case whose case officer was Deven Gadhvi. It was a no brainer that they were going to unearth the missing link this time. They were confident that the answer was in Alibaug.

At about 1:15 pm, they were received by a grateful 27-year-old sub-inspector, Mhatre, at Mandwa Beach. He had high regard for Kamble, and it was quite evident. He was driving his own police jeep and gestured the duo to the board as he got in the driving seat.

Kamble boarded in the front and asked Neel to get on from behind.

"Mhatre… listen we need to keep this hush-hush…. so here is what we will do. Do you have a private car or a motorbike or any 2 wheeler…?"

"Yes, Bhau…I have my bike at home." Mhatre was a little confused.

"Ok… see a police jeep always attracts attention. Sometimes unwarranted. So first we go to your home, park the jeep there. We have that amazing home cooked fish curry your **Aai** makes. Then we ride your bike and do our work. Classic Indian Tripling style."

It drew a chuckle out of Neel and Mhatre too who had already started the jeep and put it in motion.

"After we finish our leg work, hopefully in the evening, we will have chai pakoda at your place, and you will drop us back here in your jeep in time for the last ferry to Mumbai. Sounds like a plan, boys!!!!"

"Yes Sir!!!!"

"When is the last jetty?"

"7:30 PM, Sir."

"Perfect. We have time."

41

NOVEMBER 14TH, 2023

The men were too full to move. Neel could swear on his limited time in this life that he had not had a better fish curry before. As if they had not stuffed themselves up till throat, the halwa made the matters full to the brim. But work is work. Kamble touched the lady's feet, thanking her for food, and Neel followed suit. He led the trio out, and 3 of them settled on the bike, ready for some legwork. Mhatre had a helmet on, then Kamble, and lastly Neel, whose half-ass was hanging out and holding on to Kamble as tightly as possible.

As they were driving, Neel could see what Alibaug's appeal was. Why did this unprotected gem attract people to live out their golden years here? The beauty of the place was that it was not compartmentalised. You could not segregate the middle-class area from the gentrified area. Sandwiched between 2 hutments could be one huge mansion, which added an unmistakable character to the place. Neel was having flashes of being here before. He didn't remember he was ever here, but everything looked familiar. They crossed a couple of huge mansions that looked very familiar, and he had to ask Mhatre about them.

"The first one belongs to the most influential family of Alibaug. He had only one daughter so later it was inherited by her husband some army man…Purie something. And the second one belongs to the legend of Alibaug, the colourful Balraam pandit!" Mhatre was narrating very animatedly as if he was proud to share his town's heritage.

Neel was feeling something stronger than deja vu. But he kept his focus ahead. The bike slowed down and stopped next to a grocery store.

All 3 of them alighted with varying degrees of lethargy.

"Namaskar Mhatre saheb, is everything okay?" The shopkeeper started the conversation as soon as the helmet was off. A cop sighting, even in plain clothes, is never good news in India.

"Na Bhīma, all good. This is a senior officer from Mumbai. He wanted to ask you a few questions if that is ok." Although Bhīma clammed up almost instantly but reluctantly nodded.

Kamble was too seasoned to start immediately. He asked for 3 cigarettes and overpaid the storekeeper first. As the 3 of them lit up, Kamble was just chatting up and telling Bhīma about his own village near Aurangabad. Bhīma also showed a little more relaxed body language than before.

"Bhīma… can you see that dry patch? That small burnt up patch of land with that ruins of a hut…? Can you tell me what is the story there?" Kamble came to the point finally.

Bhīma instantly knew what was being asked here, and one could tell his guard was up.

"That is a story of extreme misfortune, Saheb*!* Destiny came and swallowed the whole family and their land in a year's time." First, the man of the house, the breadwinner, meets with an accident and dies on the spot. The bereaved wife, the single mother of 2 kids, was diagnosed with cancer in 2 month's time and was on her deathbed almost right after. The boy was 10, and the girl was 8. The grandfather was also there, but he lived outside the hut in the open.

Bhīma looked genuinely sad now.

"On the New Year night of 2010/2011, their kerosene stove blasted off, burning the whole hut. The mother and kids were charred to death, and the weak grandfather who tried to do something succumbed to his injuries in the morning. No one was spared, Saheb. No one."

There was a genuine sorrow in the narration.

"Such was the wrath of God on that land saheb that even if its empty and unclaimed, no one dares to even touch it let alone encroach it." Bhīma held his ears and mumbled something. May be praying for health and security of the family.

Kamble looked around. He could see a fancy property 100 metres across the cursed land.

"What is that? A resort or something?"

"Haan saheb, it was very popular in its days, but slowly, the curse of the land ate into its profits too. There was a time when it used to be full from November 1 to January 31. But after that incident, it got cursed, too. The guests almost vanished overnight. Still, it got booked for some weddings or parties, but around 2014-15, even that stopped. And then covid dealt the final blow. It's just locked now. This horror house was once the gorgeous ***THE ALIBAUG INN.***"

Kamble and Neel shared a glance with each other.

"Ok, Bheema…you have been extremely helpful. Tell me, how did the stove catch fire….? Accident or….?" Kamble was not looking at Bhīma directly to keep him easy and comfortable.

"It was…accident ….I mean as far as we know… I mean."

The stammering and simpering said it all.

"Why don't you ask that, Gadhvi?" An extremely frail old man came out of Bhīma's shop. He must have been sleeping on the floor all along and listening in, but he was not visible.

"Shut up baba…nothing saheb. My father just mumbles things sometimes. It's nothing. Come baba lets go inside." Bhīma greeted them and was gone inside.

Neel and Mhatre were quiet all this while just observing and listening. Neel had to say the obvious now.

"The old man made it pretty clear, Kaka. No?"

"It's not that simple, but yes, if an inquiry is initiated, then…" Kamble was kind of talking to himself.

"That is my jurisdiction bhau. I can see what are my legal options here." Said the confident Mhatre.

November 14ᵀᴴ, 2023
Mumbai, 6:00 PM

Gadhvi had reached her house. Technically, it was his house, but he liked calling it her mistress" apartment. It made him feel rich and powerful. He put the car in park and dialled Paul.

"Yes Sir…"

"Where is Kamble?"

"Sir, he has not left his house since yesterday. He must be under the weather. You don't worry, Sir. I am here all night."

"Paul…don't disturb me till I call you. Understood?"

"Sir… ji Sir."

Gadhvi then called up his family to check whether they have reached safely. He reiterated the same thing to his wife.

He could not be disturbed as he is pulling an all-nighter in office on an important case. The phone was on silent now. No sound. No vibration even.

Gadhvi rang the bell and entered the apartment to begin his night of fun.

She excused herself to go to the kitchen on the pretext of making his drink and sent a message to them.

He is here.

NOVEMBER 14ᴛʜ, 2023

Chavan Residence, 6:30 PM

The number flashing on the screen worried him. He did a quick mental math; no chance in hell this could have been good news. But good or bad, any news was important. He sighed to control his disdain for the loudmouth on the other side and accepted the call.

"Jadhav…tell me."

"Chavan Saheb…you were right. There are 2 guys from Mumbai snooping around the exact same accident site you asked me to get surveilled. They were asking a local shopkeeper Bhīma some questions too."

He was grinding his teeth hard for a minute. Fucking Gadhvi. They are just useless motherfuckers. Although he knew the answer, he still asked.

"Any names…?"

"One of them is a twenty-something boy, and the other is a cop…Kamble something…"

It took him about 30 seconds to assess what was happening, what he should do, and what the repercussions of that would be.

"Now Jadhav…listen to me… VERY…VERY… carefully because this is your chance. Your political future depends on it."

After a detailed minute-long instructional monologue, Chavan hung up. He tried to relax, but his anger was getting the better of him. He couldn't control his thoughts. His inner monologue was getting louder and louder.

Kamble was under surveillance 24/7. He had not left his house for 2 days, according to the last update. How the hell these motherfuckers missed that man stepping out. Absolutely useless. Especially that sub-inspector.

He called up Gadhvi. No answer. Again. No answer. Again.

Gadhvi had not attended 10 of his calls. The cockroach better be dead.

November 14TH, 2023
Alibaug, 7:00 PM.

After quick chai pakoda session at Mhatre residence, the trio was en route Mandwa Beach in the government jeep to board the last jetty to Mumbai. They were well on time so Mhatre was driving slow and steady. It was anyway a better option to not drive a Government Police jeep more than 30-40 clicks an hour.

"Listen Mhatre, don't go about asking everybody at the station about the case… ok. Give me a day or 2, I will check the proper legal procedure to get a closed case open. Be very careful. Not a word to anyone till then……"

Mhatre nodded in agreement.

Neel had been quiet the whole trip for a reason. His mind was playing tricks upon him ever since he got here.

Everything, every path, every building was seemingly familiar. He knew these streets. He had been here before. But why doesn't he remember clearly.

They had taken a shortcut to the port. A small dusty road through a field could save them 10 more minutes. Not that they were running late, but saving time is always a tempting idea, maybe because it has been ingrained in us that time is money.

Sunset makes you forget everything for a while. The crimson aura just silenced the 3 men with its effortless beauty. It was quite literally like riding into the sunset.

For a minute there, you don't see your troubles.

For a minute, there, you don't see the fucked up world around you.

For a minute, there, you don't see where your life is going.

For a minute there, you don't see the rear-view mirror, which clearly shows a truck cruising at easily 100 clicks an hour, zooming towards you from behind on a single-lane dusty pathway between the fields.

And when you see, it is too late.

The impact was loud and severe but diagonal because Mhatre had swerved the jeep sharply right at the last moment. The collision leapt the jeep up 10-12 feet up in the air and somersaulted once to land in the fields. The landing was cushioned by the ready for harvest crop. After one or 2 soft tumbles the vehicle came to halt.

The speeding truck was long gone.

Mhatre, Kamble, and Neel were no longer enjoying the sunset, and the duo from Mumbai were definitely going to miss their ferry back.

42
November 14ᵀᴴ, 2023

Chavan Residence, 9:30 PM

Ramesh Chavan was waiting for the call, and it came. It was Jadhav.

"It's done, Bhau. It looked like a complete accident. The truck driver has also surrendered at the police station. It's a drunken, negligent driving case. And the impact was huge and fatal in all probability."

Probability. Chavan hated that word. It reeked of chance. It reeked of dependence. It reeked of lack of control.

"What the fuck does that mean Jadhav…?"

"Bhau…all 3 were unconscious, and the jeep had landed from 20 feet leap in the air. No chance of survival. But it was important for the lorry driver to surrender to make it look like a driving under the influence case. So, he quickly drank enough and surrendered after about more than an hour…."

"And then…" Chavan was waiting for the good news.

"The police went to the accident spot and found them unconscious. But….but….still alive."

Chavan closed his eyes and took a deep breath. Useless. Absolutely useless. All of them.

"What is the latest update, Jadhav…when I say latest…it means till the last second."

"All 3 were found and ferried to Mumbai. They are currently unconscious and admitted to Trinity Hospital near the Gateway. But Chavan Saheb….trust me….they aren't going to survive……."

Chavan disconnected the call. The flip side of immense power is that one has to refrain from getting one's hand dirty. He was furious at himself that he was dependent on such nincompoops for such small things.

There was no imminent danger. The 3 of them had been in an accident. Even the driver had surrendered. But it was becoming a problem. This had to end. It must. And soon.

He called up Gadhvi again. But the bastard still didn't answer. Chavan was enraged beyond anything. He normally refrained from sending texts or anything tangible which can be traced back to him, but he was too angry to care.

He recorded a voice message and sent it across to the cockroach.

Gadhvi, you fucking idiot. You imbecile useless piece of shit. You are done. Finished. You call me as soon as you stop whoring around. Call me if you want to live to see another day. NOW.

November 14ᵀᴴ, 2023
Clarence House, 10:30 PM

It was time to worry now. That asshole Neel had promised he would be back by dinner. Shiksha has been trying his number for the past half an hour. It was unavailable. She knew the last ferry from Mandwa, Alibag, was at 7:30 PM. It should take one hour or an hour and a half max. Either way, he should have touched Mumbai by now. She started freaking out when even Kaka's number was unavailable.

Something was not right, and being the only one who knew about this trip was wearing heavy on her. It was time now. Fuck you, yaar Neel. You idiot.

Amma and Ibu were watching some mindless television. Shiksha had trouble written all over her face now. The moment Ibu saw her face, he muted the TV and gestured her to sit down next to her.

"What happened beta? What is it?" Ibu tried to sound as calm as possible.

"Cmon Shiksha, say beta….what happened?" Amma joined in.

"That… that…stupid Neel took a trip to Alibaug with Kamble Kaka. They went around noon and he promised to be back by dinner but…but…And now when I am trying to call them and no one is answering. I mean both the numbers are unreachable." Shiksha started sobbing.

Amma and Ibu glanced at each other, and something was communicated.

Amma took his phone and went to the bedroom not before patting Shiksha gently on the head as a consolation. And Ibu was sitting right next to her holding her hand.

Shiksha was surprised at the calmness on display, contrary to her worried face.

"Just relax now. You told us everything, naa. Now we will handle it."

Amma came out of the bedroom with a grim expression. Shiksha knew something was seriously wrong.

"Kamble and Neel were with a local cop on their way to Mandwa port when their jeep had a serious accident. All 3 of them are unconscious but have been ferried back to Mumbai. They are currently in the ICU of Trinity Hospital."

Amma had communicated the entire information like a zombie with a deadpan expression. It was clear he was in shock and his mind was extrapolating the most negative scenario. He can't possibly lose Neel, his only reason to live.

He sat down on the sofa, completely surrendering to gravity. A tensed Ibu and sobbing Shiksha hugged Amma from either side, but no one spoke for almost a minute.

After a tight group embrace and a good cry, they got up. Neel needed them.

Shiksha transformed herself completely in a minute, realising she couldn't afford to break down. She gave the essential meds to the oldies and packed an overnight bag for herself. There was no way she was letting Amma and Ibu stay with Neel at the hospital, and there was no way she was coming back from the hospital without Neel.

Shiksha had already called Rashmi Kaki but played down the severity of it as per Amma's instructions. They would pick her up on the way to hospital.

The news was broken to Deva, who was sleeping on the ground floor in his room. He insisted on joining but was very lovingly convinced by Amma not to. He promised they would bring Neel Baba back quickly, and they would celebrate thereafter. Meanwhile, Deva had to hold the fort at Clarence House.

They all boarded the cab, and the first thing Shiksha did was message Gau.

November 14th, 2023
Outside Kamble Residence, 11:00 PM
It had never occurred to Paul and his sidekick that it was a tad bit unusual that Kamble had not even come out of the

building once in 2 days. Not my job, he must have thought. He was not being paid to think. He was being paid to follow every order of Gadhvi saheb word by word. But he found it unusual that Kamble's wife was getting in the car with a group of people at 11 in the night, and the man didn't even bother to see her off. That was a bit unusual, and Paul thought he should inform Saheb.

He thought about it for 2 minutes before dialling but finally decided that it was important to share every piece of information in time.

He dialled Gadhvi's number, but Saheb didn't answer.

November 14ᵗʰ, 2023
Trinity Hospital, 11:45 PM.

The visitors were absolutely not allowed at this point of time under any circumstance but Rashmi Kamble played the arrogance of a senior police detectives wife with panache. The hospital staff got so scared with her power tantrums that they escorted the group to the ICU where all 3 were recuperating.

It was decided in the cab that they would remain strong and not break down, but that decision almost went out of the window the moment they entered the ICU. All 3 of the accident victims were lying in beds next to each other. Heavily bandaged. Badly swollen. Completely unconscious.

Rashmi was the first to break down. Amma and Shiksha were on either side of Neel, just looking at his whole body incredulously. Amma was just too afraid to touch him, so he ruffled his hair a little bit and kissed his forehead. Shiksha had a wave of anger coming through. She was angry at him for not including her. She promised him that she would rip him a new one the moment he was up.

The resident doctor took them aside and explained the situation. The impact was severe which initiated a lift off but the landing was cushioned by a ripe harvest.

The good news was that all 3 had regained consciousness once up till now. They were right now in deep sleep because of a strong dosage of morphine. They will be checked early tomorrow morning for fractures, muscle tears and concussion. But prima facie, the doctor went ahead and pronounced all of them lucky. They were lucky indeed to be alive because it could have been a lot worse. Although doctors never commit to such things prematurely, the group convinced him to say it. All of them were out of danger.

"There can be no one in the ICU for the night. We will take them for tests at 8 in the morning and move them to rooms thereafter. Only then you can be with them. So please go home tonight and come back at 10 am in the morning."

The doctor knew what he had just said was absolutely futile. No one was going. No one ever does.

The group went into the canteen, and Amma gave the group tea and coffee.

"What the hell happened?" Shiksha was the first one to poke the elephant in the room.

Amma and Ibu had no idea, so of course, all eyes and ears were on Rashmi.

"I mean, I don't know if Neel was going to be there, but Rachit was certainly being weird for a couple of days." Rashmi controlled her sobbing.

"Weird in what way?" Ibu handed a paper napkin to her.

"I mean, 2 days in a row, Rachit stepped out of the house dressed as a teenager with shorts, a T-shirt, shades and a cap.

When I teased him about it, he brushed it off as undercover work. I didn't pry much, you know. It was quite funny, and I didn't take it that seriously……"

Amma and Ibu looked at each other because they knew this meant the Kamble household was being surveilled, and someone had seen them picking up Rashmi an hour back.

Shiksha convinced Rashmi to go back because of kids. And she invoked the caring gentlemen in Amma and Ibu who will not allow Rashmi to go back alone at this hour. The gentlemen duo agreed.

Shiksha held Amma's hand a bit longer and pressed it hard.

"I am here. If he is up, I will know immediately because I am not going anywhere. I will call you, Amma, if anything comes up. Go. Take rest and come back at 10 tomorrow."

Amma kissed Shiksha on the forehead, and the group left.

43
November 15th, 2023

Mumbai, 1:30 AM

Every upper one takes is followed by a massive natural downer. Balance of nature. Gadhvi got up with a metallic taste in his mouth. The performance-enhancement drug he took knocked him out cold. The girl was sleeping next to him. He got up, yearning for water. His parched mouth was craving moisture. He refused to admit, meanwhile, that he was too old for this shit.

He downed the whole bottle from the fridge. He casually picked up his phone while his temples were playing table tennis.

And then his head exploded as if the game of table tennis in his head upgraded from table tennis to mortal combat to say the least.

Ten missed calls from Chavan. A call from Paul. And the voice mail was the last straw.

His fingers were trembling as he dialled Chavan's number.

"Hello *saheb*....I... I....actually...."

"You slimy turd....Gadhvi...you are a cockroach, and I will crush you under my chappal. Now, if you want to live...

forget anything else…just live…you listen to me ….VERY. VERY…carefully…"

Chavan drilled for the next 5 minutes into Gadhvi's ear, which brought his entire lineage out of the grave. He finally gave some instructions, which Gadhvi promised to follow to the T.

Gadhvi took his overnight bag and left the apartment banging the door hard behind him. He didn't care. Never did.

The elevator went to the P2 level, where his car was parked.

PLOP PLOP

He placed his bag in the boot. Closed the door, and ***Thud Thud Thud.***

His head was not hurting anymore. His headache was gone all of a sudden. He was lying down on the floor. All relaxed. Maybe because he was dead.

The cause of death was REPEATED BLUNT FORCE TRAUMA MAJORLY TO THE BACK OF SKULL & the PLAUSIBLE MURDER WEAPON: THE WOUND SUGGEST A HEAVY BAT/HAMMER WITH PROTRUSIONS AT THE BUSINESS END. IT COULD BE BARBED WIRE METALLIC BEARINGS OR GEMSTONES.

They picked up his body and stuffed it in the trunk of his car. A placard was stuffed in his mouth. The placard one finds in the cricket stadium for audiences to cheer their batsmen with. A placard which just had one thing printed on it - **the number 6.**

44.

NOVEMBER 15ᵀᴴ, 2023

Chavan Residence, 2:00 AM

Ramesh Chavan was not sleeping. He was trying to calm down but couldn't. There were way too many loose ends. His primary thought right now was the future promise he was making to himself or maybe indirectly to God. Once this mess gets cleared, he will live differently. But how? His trust quotient in his team was at an all-time low. Bloody team of foot soldiers – useless. That Jadhav in Alibaug – useless. And above all, the incompetent cockroach Gadhvi is useless. Utterly useless. His phone rang and flashed Gadhvi calling. Remember the idiot and the idiot calls.

Less than an hour back he gave an earful and future plan of action to that cockroach and now he is calling again. He really wished in that moment that Gadhvi was dead. You know what they say, be careful what you wish for.

"What is it now? This better be good, Gadhvi...." Thundered Chavan.

There was silence at the other end. Just a sound of soft breathing.

Ramesh Chavan made it this far in life because he never assumed things. He believed only what he saw. But right now, he was sure who was on the other line somehow. And it wasn't Gadhvi.

"Hello……"

"Long time Chavan… It's been almost 13 years, huh…"

Sometimes, 2 people who have never met and never spoken to each other know each other deeply. They know what the other one is thinking. Chavan's heart rate was elevated. His breathing was heavy and hard. He knew in his heart this day would come someday. But here it was, and he didn't know how to react. But years and years of being a ruthless politician, the training kicked in. He knew it was time for an all-out offence now. And the rage started building up in him.

"Listen motherfucker… do you know who I am? What can I do… huh… You have a death wish…I…." Chavan was now mad with rage as the words were frothing out of his mouth.

"Shhh….shhh….You are a smart man. You know you have to listen right now. You know angry people make bad decisions. Calm down Chavan Saheb."

The calmness in the voice was eerie. But Chavan knew that the other guy was right. If he had dared to call after so many years then it was important to listen now. Chavan controlled his breathing and there was a silence for a moment at both ends.

"Good. Now listen carefully point by point……Number - 1…Gadhvi is obviously dead, stuffed in the boot of his car, which is parked in the basement of his Versova flat. Number - 2….you will use your power and send some cleanup squad there and retrieve the body of that creep…"

"Listen…you don't realise……" Chavan interrupted.

"SHUT THE FUCK UP!" The voice boomed at an insane decibel level, and Chavan was actually taken aback a little. He knew if the guy on the other side had the courage to call his personal number and threaten the sitting Home Minister of a state, there must be something. He should listen now. He had to.

"Number - 3… you will plant Gadhvi's body at his home and make it look like an unfortunate accident. A heavily drunk Gadhvi slipped and hit his head. Fatally. His family was out of the station, so no immediate assistance could be administered…blah… blah…blah….you know the drill. This must be a piece of cake……"

This time there was no interruption from Chavan's side instead his mind was racing. Where is the leverage. Why so confident? What does he have?

"Number - 4… The shoddy investigation report of the Alibaug accident made by Gadhvi and some testimonies can initiate an inquiry. Remember, Chavan, you don't need to be proven guilty….people should just think you are and you are dead politically." The confidence in the voice was worrisome.

Chavan was nervous now and a little bit impressed, actually. He kept quiet.

"Number - 5….Kanupriya Chavan."

Chavan was hit with a bolt of lightning. He couldn't speak up even if he wanted to.

"The apple of your eye. Your only child. Your princess - Kanupriya Chavan, is studying at Wharton. Right?"

Chavan was completely deflated now.

"Listen…Sir…this is not right….she is innocent… please…"

"Innocent…right…wrong…These words don't suit you motherfucker….this. Now is not the time and place to have a moral debate about right and wrong… The right time was 13 years ago, and the right place was Alibaug. So just listen…"

Chavan was feeling something strange. Something new……this was helplessness.

"Now where was I… yes….Kanupriya Chavan. We know her apartment. We know her car. We know her daily schedule. We know her every hangout. She is actually being watched as we speak. We monitor her every move, Chavan. Now, if what I told you is not done at the earliest… Chavan, you don't know … how pure an emotion revenge is. Lastly and most importantly, if you try to hurt Kamble, that boy or anyone else involved, I will extract your daughter's fingernails one at a time and send you by mail. It is a promise, and I am a man of my word. Now get to work, or she will pay for the sins of her father."

Another strange feeling was developing in Chavan's heart. Something even newer. It was regret.

NOVEMBER 15TH, 2023
Trinity Hospital, Mumbai, 10:30 AM.

All the necessary tests were done on all the victims. A few broken ribs, some minor concussions and a few broken bones. It's not a bad scenario, given the intent behind the collision. All 3 were now moved to their respective rooms to recover. They were all bandaged and strapped, and the verdict was that they would spend the night in the hospital. If all goes well, all 3 of them can be discharged the next morning, and recovery can continue in the more comfortable space of home with frequent checkups, of course.

Neel had a fracture in his left arm and heavy swelling on the right side of his face. He was lying at an angle, resting it out as for the past 3 hours, he had undergone all essential tests and was exhausted. Shiksha was by his side all along, and she had already given Amma all the updates. She had also made a case for them to come after lunch because Neel was quite exhausted and in and out of sleep now. Neither of them had said a word till now, but Shiksha was holding his right hand clasped tightly between her palms, and she had no intention to let go.

Rachit Kamble entered the room, walking like a zombie with a helping cane. He had a heavily bandaged face as the glass shards had cut him badly. Broken ribs, bruised shoulder, and fractured arm were a few troubles Kamble was carrying.

He acknowledged Shiksha and went straight to Neel. With tears in his eyes, he gently caressed Neel's hair and said, *"Sorry yaar."*

Neel tried to move his neck in disagreement and lifted his fractured but free hand and gave Kaka a thumbs up while Shiksha was smiling tearfully at the reunion.

"Ok, boys, enough now. Kaka, I spoke to Rashmi Kaki; she is on her way. And please go to your room and rest now. There is enough time later to catch up."

Kamble turned around to go out. Shiksha quickly rushed to his aid and steered him towards the door. Neel was trying to say something in a feeble voice, which made them turn around.

"Kaka….this was not an accident." Shiksha and Kamble had turned around completely with their back towards the door. They had not noticed Rashmi enter quietly.

"I know Neel, and trust me…… I am going find those sons of bitches and…"

"And do what ……you fucking Kamble!! Think about your son and this bitch first and then those sons of bitches…"

A tearful and angry Rashmi rushed in and embraced Kamble.

Nothing needed to be said.

The couple in love staggered out.

Shiksha was laughing at the comical cuteness of the couple as she came back and sat next to Neel clasping his right hand tightly with hers.

"I am sorry Shiksha" Shiksha kissed his hand and for a second it felt that there were just 2 people in the whole world. Neel had never felt such wave of any emotion before. For a moment there, Neel wanted to plant his lips on Shiksha's but decided against it. He was on a lot of medication and his breath could kill a goat he thought. Shiksha broke his trance.

"So what actually happened there?"

Neel told every single detail about his Alibaug trip and the speeding truck behind them.

"So you think someone was spooked that you were there, huh…."

Neel nodded in agreement, and before he could say something, there was a knock on the door.

It was Gaurang Bedi.

NOVEMBER 15TH, 2023
Gadhvi Residence, 11:00 AM.

She always prayed before coming to this house. She was dreading especially today. She knew that Madam was out for a day and she prayed for that creep to not be there while she cleaned and cooked around the house. She had seen many creepy leering husbands in her line of work as a housemaid but this policeman was the filthiest pig she had seen. It was as if being a top cop had given him a licence to touch anybody anywhere, anytime.

Her dread was turning into happiness because she had rung the bell 5 times now. No answer. Madam had given her a duplicate key for this very purpose. She decided to go in and do the chores as fast as possible. It was just for today. From tomorrow, Madam will be there.

She opened the door and went in. An audible sigh of relief came out of her as she walked through the living room which quickly transformed into a stifled scream.

The creep was lying down on the kitchen floor in a pool of blood.

As she returned to her senses, she shouted at top of her lungs and rightfully raised an alarm. As the neighbours came running, she was standing in one corner shaking like a leaf.

From what she was hearing, a pang of disappointment took over the initial shock. She was disappointed that she didn't pray for a pot of gold because it looked like her casual prayer was answered.

The creepy cop was dead.

November 15ᵀᴴ, 2023
Trinity Hospital, Mumbai, 11:30 AM

It was too long a period of pleasantries and rudimentary chitchat. Where did it hurt? How did it happen? Does it pain a lot? What are doctors saying? What really happened in Alibaug? The 3 musketeers were not on their game. Something was off. And then Neel said…

"Gau… were you actually in Pune at your grandmother's place because you were upset with me, or did you find some cute boy and you were off to a steamy getaway, huh?"

Shiksha burst out laughing at this completely unexpected jab.

"Oh please ….Neel …you are not that important to me *chutiye*….You were right. I met someone. I was out there having a steamy getaway……you… you…"

Gau could not finish it. He broke down and carefully hugged Neel.

"I love you yaar Neel."

"I love you too, Gau. And I am sorry……that……"

"I know. It's ok. It was time to…….so…."

Shiksha jumped into the conversation. "Why do you love this narcissistic asshole Gau? I am curious."

Shiksha's playfulness was met with a sombre and sincere-looking face by Gau.

"I came out to my parents that very day, Shiksha. They are still awkward and distraught. I came out to my sister. She is still awkward. Don't even get me started on my grandparents. My whole family who loves me are basically being a complete asshole to me. But this Neel Mantri, he was a narcissistic asshole then, and he is a narcissistic asshole now. That's why I love him. He never changed."

For a second, there was a heavy silence, eventually broken by Neel.

"Umm….I am not sure how to respond here. I am not coming off well in that monologue."

Laughter all around. And it was interrupted by Rachit Kamble.

The look on Kamble's face brought laughter to an instant halt. He was solemn and dead serious.

"Neel….IGP Gadhvi was found dead in his house about an hour ago. On the face of it, he must have died last night.

An autopsy is awaited, but it looks like he slipped into a drunken stupor and hit his head. Died instantly."

There was dead silence in the room.

"Kaka…was the wound identical to other victims?"

"Yes, but…the corner of a heavy wrought iron centre table near the kitchen looks good for it."

"Ok…is there any sign which suggests…victim number 6?"

"Umm… no. No number 6 or anything. Nothing of that sort. It really looks like an accident, Neel."

Neel thought for a moment.

"Kaka…is Mhatre still here…?"

"Yes … Why?"

"I need to meet with him and get something checked. I think it's time to finish this now."

45

DECEMBER 31ST, 2010

Alibaug, 6:00 PM

"**B**hīma Kaka! Bhīma Kaka! Please come na! Maa is coughing blood non-stop. Please Bhīma Kaka…!" The 12-year-old Shiva was banging on the door of the shop non-stop.

Bhīma was getting ready for his cigarette stall duty for the night at **The Alibaug Inn.** It was New Year's Eve, and the upper middle class from Mumbai flocked to the fancy resort for the celebrations. He never understood why. It was time for an additional expense of a new calendar; what is the need to celebrate? Anyway, it was their money. Even after bribing 500 rupees to the night manager, Bhīma would make double what he makes with his shop in a week by selling cigarettes in the resort tonight. So, wearing a formal shirt and trousers was no big deal. It was just for tonight. He had to set up shop at 6, actually, and he was already running late. On top of that, this neighbour kid is bashing the door.

"What is the matter with you, Shiva? You want to break my damn door?"

"Bhīma Kaka, please come urgently. Maa….maa…. is…." And he ran to his house, imploring Bhīma to follow.

Bhīma knew about his mother's disease, so he instantly ran behind the boy.

The poor woman was coughing non-stop, and with each cough came a little smattering of fresh blood. Her eight-year-old daughter was sitting beside her. Unresponsive. Praying may be. The extremely frail father-in-law was sitting outside the house with both hands on his head. Helpless. Completely helpless.

Bhīma took out his mobile phone. He remembered he had some balance left for outgoing. He could call the local doctor, and he did. Bhīma knew he was running late, but there was no functioning adult in this household. He started working on the apology he would render to the resort manager for the delay. It was a very simple apology. Extra 500 rupees. Bhīma did some calculations and made his peace with it.

The local doctor came on his battered motorcycle in 15 mins. He had been here before for the very same reason, so he came prepared. Instantly, he administered a lifesaving injection to the woman and a strong dosage of morphine, which would let her rest till the next day early morning.

"Bhīma… if she is not hospitalised in Mumbai soon she will….you know… very soon" There was nothing complicated to say or understand there. It was pretty clear. It had been pretty clear for a couple of months now.

The doctor left, and Bhīma was worried about what they would eat for dinner.

"Listen, Shiva, I am going to the resort to work. Come with me. Do an odd job here and there, and I will arrange dinner for your family. Ok.

"Ok, Bhīma. Thank you for your kindness." He went closer to his little sister and gently patted her head. "Chutki,

Take care of Daadu and Maa; I will be back soon with some food."

Bhīma's eyes swelled up at this brazen display of unadulterated innocence and love. Poverty is the most dreadful disease in this world, he thought.

The Alibaug Inn was the most coveted New Year's Eve destination on the outskirts of Mumbai. The ferry ride from Gateway of India gave the journey a magical feel, and that made the destination even more interesting. Every year, it was jam-packed on December 31st, and today was no exception.

Bhīma used his minuscule influence and 1000 rupees upfront to the manager and got Shiva a petty job of cleaning the dishes. He was promised dinner for 4 and some petty cash for that petty job. The boy could take a break from 9:30 to 10:30, where he could go back home with dinner and then work the dishes till the kitchen was running. The family will not sleep on an empty stomach tonight. One day at a time, Bhīma thought.

DECEMBER 31ST, 2010
Alibaug, 11:45 PM

The party at the resort was in full swing as it was just 15 minutes to midnight. Drinks were flowing, music was loud, and patrons were dancing like no one was watching, which was true, actually. No one was watching as pretty much everybody was flying in friendly skies. The kids accompanying the adults were being catered to by a separate entertainment unit. There were clowns, jugglers, magicians. The kids were pretty occupied with the show. Shiva was constantly watching all this from the kitchen window as he was scrubbing the cutlery with his little hands. His empty eyes could just watch the difference, disparity and distinction between the 2 worlds, seemingly separated by just a window. He quietly cried inside his heart, killed his desire to be outside with other kids, and just turned around to face the kitchen wall. He turned his back towards the outer world just like they did to him.

The party had reached its crescendo as the countdown had begun. As the number 1 was announced and the clock struck 12, a confetti blast engulfed the open garden area of celebration. Music was blasting, and people were wishing each other a Happy New Year. Just as it always happens, now, when the clock had struck 12, and the big event had panned out, everybody was more relaxed and stationed. The buffet was winding up, and the last order of drinks was being served. The music was dim and ambient now. The fun from the community level had now become localised to individual groups and their tables.

There was a small bit of a magician performing card tricks from table to table for generous tips. Shiva saw an opportunity to earn some extra bucks here and there. He quickly ran to the secluded corner where only 3 tables were there, and the magician had not reached them yet. One table was occupied by 2 couples, the second had a group of 4 decent and kind-looking older gentlemen, and the third was occupied by a rather rowdy group of 6 people. Shiva noticed a couple of waiters standing by all the time for the third table, which clearly meant that's where the money was. They had a leader who was dressed in all white from head to toe and wearing huge gold chains. He looked rich and powerful.

"Sir, Sir….can I show some magic to you…some entertainment, Sir…"

Although the boy clearly addressed the third group, the tables were not that far off, so the occupants of the other 2 tables also heard the proposal and cheered the cuteness and innocence of the little magician. The rowdy group reluctantly agreed. Shiva knelt down in front of the rowdy group leader, who was a bit amused.

"So you know magic huh little boy....let's see your magic..." The group laughed. The occupants of other 2 table had brought their chairs closer now and it became a big group. The little boy had their attention.

Shiva mumbled a small prayer in his heart and began.

"Choose a number, Sir… a single digit number… not zero, please… and please don't tell me or anyone else…"

After a stifled laughter, the leader played along.

"Ok….done…now…?"

"Now… multiply that number with 9, Sir…"

"Hmmm…ok…done."

"Now the product must be a double digit number Sir, kindly add the 2 digits of that number please …."

"Oh, come on, this is not magic. This is elementary mathematics. *Saheb,* it's a buzzkill." One of the entourage members slurred.

There were other voices of dissent from the group as well, but the leader played along. He could see other people from neighbouring tables had also tuned in. The politician inside him decided to play nice for the gallery. The boy's trick will fall flat, but he would still give him some money, and that's it.

"Ok Ok done…I added the 2 digits of the double digit number I got as the product. Now?"

"Very well, Sir…the sum you have from adding the 2 digits, please subtract 5 from it now."

"Umm….done"

The boy stood up and started walking slowly, exhibiting classy showmanship.

"Now, my good Sir, whatever number remains with you after subtracting 5 - map it to the corresponding alphabet. For if it's 1, then A; if it's 2, then B; if it's 3, then C….and so on."

One of the rowdy group members had already taken out a 500 rupee note and kept it ready. He gestured to the waiter for another round of drinks.

"Yes… done…I have my alphabet. Now what …"

"Now please think of the name of a country which starts with that alphabet letter Sir… not a town…not a city…A country, Sir. Country."

Now obviously the people from other 2 tables who had chimed in were active participants in the trick. They had performed every single instruction the boy had given to the gentleman clad in all white in their own minds and were eagerly waiting for the epilogue. The climax!

"Ok, little boy…I thought of a country starting with that letter……Now?"

"Well, now, Sir…Welcome to Denmark!!!!!"

The leader's mouth was gaping open, and anybody could see that the boy had read his mind.

The loud cheers followed, one of the bigger guys from adjoining table hoisted the boy and planted him on the table. And everybody started complimenting him. The leader was not happy. His fragile ego took a minor beating. He was just quiet trying to figure out in his head what just happened.

"Very good …very good. Here is a 100 for you, my boy, and here is a 500 waiting in my shirt pocket if you can…read my mind again."

"Sure, Sir. My honour." The boy jumped down and stood in front of the leader again.

"Can I make a little change here and there to make it more interesting Sir?" The boy asked after taking position.

"Yes, go ahead." The leader lit a cigarette.

"Choose a number ….single digit number and multiply it……."

"Yeah yeah…multiply it with 9. Add the 2 digits of the double digit product and then subtract 5 from the sum……" The leader was irritated.

"Not quite, Sir…why repeat the trick. Repetition is boring. Let's change a bit, shall we?"

Shiva was exhibiting supreme showmanship. The audience was clapping and cheering.

"Multiply it with 9, add the digits of the double-digit product and … um… this time, please subtract 4 from the sum, Sir."

"Done"

"And now think the corresponding …"

"Yeah …yeah… done. I have the corresponding alphabet."

"Ummm….think of your favourite bird whose name starts with that alphabet….yes bird, my good Sir….starting with that letter…."

"Done."

Shiva started to move his outstretched arms like a bird walking around and mimicking the flying.

"You are an Eagle, Sir…"

The leader stared the boy for a second and gave him the 500 rupees and stood up. The crowd was stifling their laughter as the leader's face was red with anger. He crushed his cigarette rather animatedly under the heels of his pointy and shiny white shoes. Ramesh Chavan was boiling with rage as he stormed out. The rowdy gang cursed the boy and followed him.

The audience was screaming and howling and doing high fives with Shiva. There were some generous tips floating around and finally after everybody left, Shiva was sitting with the 4 elderly gentlemen and was busy counting his money.

He made about 2000 rupees there. He kissed the money, threw a salute and a flying kiss to God above and pocketed the cash.

"What will you do with that money, Shiva?" one of the 4 older gentlemen asked.

"First, I will get my mother treated at the best hospital in Mumbai. We will leave tomorrow itself. Once my mother is getting well, I will buy a pink bicycle for my sister and a gold necklace. I would also enrol her in the best school in Mumbai. Oh, I forgot, I will also have to get Daadu to the same hospital so that I can monitor both of them, you know. Also, I would rent a flat near the hospital till my mother and Daadu get better and my sister can go to school. I mean I can only rent because I wouldn't be able to buy one. Houses are expensive in Mumbai, I read in the newspaper. And lastly, I would put the remaining money in a bank like grown-ups do. And also, I would give some money to Bhīma to help our family today."

Everyone was speechless because they were choked up with this blissful display of innocence. Such unbridled love for family and unadulterated purity of intent broke every heart present there. The older gentlemen were just quiet and trying hard not to well up. Unsuccessfully.

"And what about you… Shiva…you don't want anything for yourself?" Said one of the gentlemen with a heavy voice.

"No. I don't need anything. I am happy if my family is happy."

The boy pocketed the cash, wished everyone Happy New Year and trotted off.

JANUARY 1ST, 2011
Alibaug, 2:30 AM

It was not Ramesh Chavan's usual gang. These were just some ambitious people with high aspirations and low moral compass who happened to recognise the rising political star in the resort and just wanted to hang with him and get into his good books. Ramesh Chavan was drunk on power, and the other 5 were drunk on greed. And all of them were drunk on enough liquor not to think clearly and rationally. A megalomaniac was hurt; his pride was hurt in front of a group of people by a boy. A poor, downtrodden, insignificant waste of space, boy. How can a person in his position accept that? Ramesh Chavan was not having it.

The group stealthily crossed the field and were behind the hut. The Daadu was sleeping in the front and his infrequent cries were barely audible. The 5 men entourage completely blinded with borrowed ego sprinkled the hut generously with kerosene. Lots and lots of kerosene as Ramesh Chavan watched them. He just stood there smoking as the men were done and were now standing beside him. He mumbled something.

"You know, smart boy, Choose a single-digit number. Multiply it by 9. Add the digits of the double-digit product. And subtract 3 out of the sum this time. Let's do something different, Sir. Lastly, map the remaining number to its corresponding alphabet. That would be F, wouldn't it? And now think of my favourite thing starting with the letter F..."

Chavan took a deep drag and exhaled audibly.

"It's fucking fire...."

And just like in movies, he flicked his burning cigarette onto the top of the hut covered with husk and chaff. It took less than a minute for the hut to become a giant bowl of fire. Nobody inside even had a chance to get out.

The poor grandfather couldn't even shout for help. The helpless old man tried to go inside and help but collapsed with smoke inhalation and got badly burnt.

The mother inside, his sister and Shiva got burnt alive along with the 2000 rupees he had earned that night.

46
NOVEMBER 19ᵀᴴ, 2023

Clarence House, *7:30 AM*

It had been 3 days since Neel was home nursing his broken body. The swellings had begun to subside now, and recovery was faster than expected, all thanks to Ms. Shiksha Sheikh and Mr. Deva. Neel was walking fine now but had not been sleeping well. The unresolved story was stuck in his mind, but it was all going to change today. India was playing Australia to win their third ODI World Cup. The Indian Team had momentum, confidence, talent - you name it. Neel knew India was winning. That was not the reason he was restless. Neel had been up since 4:30 in the morning, dreading the truth. He spoke to Kamble Kaka last night. The forensic analysis of Eknath Patil's wig was done, and the reports confirmed what Neel had dreaded. He had an early morning call with the fellow victim, Mhatre, who took 2 days but finally confirmed Neel's suspicion. He was dreading it but was right again.

Shiksha came in with turmeric milk instead of coffee, the age-old Indian talisman of healing.

"Arey… you are up again, Neel. At least lie down, please. Do you know how strong those painkillers are? You have to rest for longer periods of time, or you will be disoriented.

What is it with you? Why are you fighting the meds? Can you tell me if something is bothering you, Neel?"

Neel couldn't tell her that he wished he was sleeping because he wanted all of this to be a dream. Not real. Not happening. But facts don't lie.

He made Shiksha sit on the corner of the bed with her back against the wall, put his head in her lap and closed his eyes. He was snoring softly in less than a minute.

NOVEMBER 19ᵀᴴ, 2023
Kamble Residence, 8:30 AM

Kamble felt that the entire juggernaut of events had just come to a screeching halt. The special investigation team had declared IGP Gadhvi's death an accident, which was a no-brainer for him. There was already a replacement for Gadhvi, who had deprioritised all of Kamble's cases and very politely commended him for good work and suggested time off for as long as required for complete recovery. He was relieved, for he was not sure what was the truth anymore. Somebody went to the length of killing 2 cops and a boy just because of a visit. Was Ramesh Chavan behind that? He would never be able to prove that; the trail would end somewhere abruptly for sure. He couldn't imagine what skeletons were being stopped from getting unearthed.

It was as if what forensic analysis of the wig Neel requested to get done was not weird enough; what was weirder was that it came back positive. What did that boy know and was not telling him?

He made a mental note to ask at the evening mehfil. He would not drink, but he was still going to celebrate India's World Cup victory. And he was already dreaming about the food.

November 19ᵀᴴ, 2023
Clarence House, 10:30 AM

It was the usual breakfast table. Amma and Ibu were having their chai and discussing the ideal combination for the Indian and Australian teams today. This was it. Indian Men's team had a flawless World Cup campaign reminiscent of the mighty Australians in the late 90s and early 2000s. It had all come down to today. The winner takes all. This is what they play for, and this is why we watch. Ultimate glory.

"Amma…what say we knock a few down at the rink? It's the tradition!" Neel was feeling a little better after the nap.

"Are you crazy? Of course not! Amma, look at this idiot….He is in no condition to walk, let alone play. Are you out of your mind?" Shiksha was furious, darting in and out of the dining area.

"Oh Shiksha, I will not ball or even roll my arm. I will just stand and throw for Amma to knock a few. That's all. It's for good luck, yaar. It's the final today. The final."

Amma had been quiet all this while. He looked at Ibu, nodded his head and smiled. Something was communicated which only they understood. And may be Neel.

"Let's go champ. Come. Let's knock a few for good luck."

Amma geared up while Neel was checking the balls. There were a dozen shining red cherries stuffed in the netted stocking, ripe for the picking. And there was another dozen which were a little used.

"Amma, where are the old balls? You bought a new packet already."

"Yes… the older olds were thrown out. The older new are new olds now. Wow. That is a sentence I never thought I would use." Amma took the guard.

Neel was interested in examining the new and old.

"But why throw them out?"

"You said they were deformed and a bit askew, right?"

Neel made up his mind. He picked up a brand new one for the current session. And thus, the duel began. Grandfather vs Grandson. It was just the 2 of them. No one else. It was between them now.

Amma knew his grandson so well that he knew what was coming. "Don't hold back, Neel. It's time."

It was as if Neel understood very clearly what was being said here.

"How did you know it was Ramesh Chavan who burnt the hut?" Neel tossed the ball up for drift.

Amma was ready. He stretched out and blunted it.

"Bhīma and Bhīma's father saw them leave from the site. There were kerosene containers all over the place. Those containers were removed, and Gadhvi converted the arson into an accident. The father-son duo were actually eyewitnesses." Amma took the guard again.

Neel planned a straight one in his head.

"Why not go to the police, I mean the superiors?" Neel took a moment.

"Even the good cops are by the book. The area was completely sanitised even before the sunrise. There was no evidence at all. And eyewitnesses didn't want to come forward. Chavan was the rising star then. We discussed, and it was a futile exercise."

Amma was looking dead straight into Neel's eyes and talking.

"We?" Neel fired a quick one.

Amma was ready. "Ibu, Balli, Deva and I."

"Whose idea was it to turn vigilantes then?" Neel gathered the ball.

"It was all of us. We all lived together here at Clarence House at that time. I mean you. We had that tragic loss just a month back. Everything was broken. We were in Alibaug just for the night of New Year's for a change of scenery, and we came back even scarred."

Amma was looking down at the pitch while talking. He saw a weed plant mushrooming in the pitch. He went ahead and uprooted it.

There was a longer pause as if Amma was reliving the moment. He was swivelling the bat in his hands as if trying to find apt words to describe his feelings.

"A 12-year-old boy lost his father and was soon to lose his mother. There was a frail grandfather almost already in the grave and an 8-year-old little girl. Just the mere mention of the family elicits sympathy, right? How can this group of people be a threat to anyone, Neel? Why kill something that is half dead already? Why?"

Neel was listening in rapt attention and watched Amma wipe off a couple of tears and clear his throat.

"You were not well, Neel. After almost a month, you were sleeping soundly, so we let you be in the room right across the lawn where we were. You should have seen the boy, Neel. Showing little mathematical tricks with showmanship and panache. He reminded me of you. The exact same spark in the eyes. And his love for the family – you should have seen it!"

Neel noticed the change in Amma's expressions. He saw the fossils of his jawline clench, and his grip on the handle of the bat got stronger.

"We must have been with him for half an hour, but his personality broke through. That innocence, that purity, that spirit – it was supposed to be preserved, protected and nurtured. He was supposed to be given wings to fly. He was capable of doing great things, Neel, just like you."

"He deserved compassion.

He deserved some empathy.

He deserved a chance."

Amma was in a trance now. His voice and body language was seriously loud now.

"But no…he was burnt alive along with a defenceless family. For what? Because he was showing some harmless tricks? A slimy scum of the Earth political worm felt offended because the boy showed a little showmanship at his cost? They burnt an ailing woman, a little girl and a boy - ALIVE!!!"

"BURNT ALIVE, Neel, BURNT ALIVE!!!!!!

HOW DARE THEY.!!!!!!

They all deserve to die and rot in hell. ALL OF THEM. EACH AND EVERY ONE OF THEM!"

Amma was trembling with anger and his decibel level had touched dangerous levels. Neel was a little shell-shocked at this sudden and unexpected burst of intensity by Amma, and frankly a little scared too. Ibu and Deva came running because they knew what was happening already. They held Amma tight and recomposed him.

The trio was just quiet and huddled together tightly. Amma was quiet now. He caught his breath.

"I am fine. I am fine. C'mon, Neel, bowl me some spins and put some revs on it. Don't take a run-up. Just stand and deliver."

Neel went to the mark. Amma took the guard while Ibu and Deva were standing on the sidelines, which were very close to traditional first slip and leg slip positions.

"Yes, so… where was I? We couldn't sleep after that night. None of us. We were boiling with rage. All of us. That boy – his smile, his innocence was haunting us. And then it was just decided….mutually within the group that…" Amma was falling short of words.

"That sometimes execution and extermination is the only answer." Ibu finished for him.

Neel was in utter disbelief. He gripped the ball hard and gave as many revolutions on the ball as he could. The extra effort made him wince in pain. Amma completely missed that one on the pads.

"Howzzat!!!"

"Missing leg, not out."

Neel was back at the mark.

Neel had to ask now. Everything.

"It was Chavan. He was the monster behind the massacre. What about the others? Were they not as culpable, or did they deserve it too? I mean even Eknath Patil?"

"Yes, they deserved it too." It was Ibu. He continued.

"They were there. They had a choice then. They took blood money and disappeared and vowed silence. They could have not. They had a choice. They made their choice. We made ours."

Neel could not believe it was Ibu talking.

"Also, Neel Baba, Eknath was the last one to go because he had transformed his life, unlike others. We were divided about him till the last moment. But he was there, and he made a choice. He had to go." It was Deva. Neel's favourite person in the world. Deva, the nurturer. Deva, the gentlest soul on Earth. Neel would not have believed had he not been witnessing this.

The trinity of justice had spoken. The 3 of them were on one side, and Neel was on the other side. Alone. So far.

"Oh, everyone is here…" The stare-off was broken by Shiksha.

"I am going to go see my friend for coffee. Poor girl had an ugly break-up. I will be back for the match, guys. Neel, please go rest now. I am serious. Enough knocks for good luck. Ammmaaa…"

"Yes yes… Neel. C'mon. Enough. Let's go upstairs. Come I will fix some turmeric milk for you and Deva will fix our chai."

There was a small break in the convention before the group reconvened at the dining table outside the kitchen.

"When did it start?" Neel was blowing soft air. The milk was hot.

"After a restless 2-3 months, we were sure we couldn't continue living with the knowledge and do nothing. Something needed to be done. And then Balraam Pandit said…" Amma paused for a sip of his tea.

"Let's kill them all one by one." Ibu finished what Amma started.

There was a long silence after that declaration. There had to be. It was Amma's turn now to ask.

"When did you first know Neel?"

"It was the dates to begin with. The dates of… umm… execution, the modus operandi of execution and the counting of execution with subtle clues - it all bothered me. I knew there was something deep running there. But I couldn't figure out the connection at all. And then……"

Neel finished his milk, made a grotesque face and continued.

"Then Col. Purie happened. I was sure it was just a distraction. It was all neatly tied with a bow on top. The convenient murder weapon. The surveillance pictures. And the killer was dead now. End of story. How convenient." Neel maybe smiled a little there.

Amma and Ibu had their faces turn grim and solemn at the mention of Colonel Purie.

"It was all Colonel's idea. We have always been friends with him, especially Pandit. Pandit shared our pursuit of justice with him when he was diagnosed with terminal cancer. He was on our side in a minute. Military mind and heart cannot withstand injustice." Amma took a beat of silence to honour his friend's memory. Like always, Ibu picked up from where Amma trailed off.

"It was Colonel's idea. When he knew the time was near, we all met. It was after the deadliest pandemic wave had passed. He said his entire life was for upholding the integrity of his country, and he would be honoured if his death could also contribute to a noble cause. What a man!"

Ibu choked up.

"My mind started to race when Shiksha found Asif's picture with Colonel's son Aashish. The Colonel was close to Balli's uncle. Alibaug connection. And you guys and Balli's uncle. It all pointed……somewhere…"

They were waiting for him to continue.

"Once I had the bug in my head, I jotted down everything weird around the group. Your group. I had zoned out my memories of that Alibaug trip because I had deleted that year from my memory. But it came rushing back….the year…. after Maa had gone….the Alibaug trip….2010 New Year's Eve. All was reinforced when I remembered you all were there in Alibaug for New Year's Eve. The very foundation of the case was Alibag in 2010/11. Then it was the case of the balls……."

Amma and Ibu laughed out loud.

"Why the balls? Why the dates?" Neel was getting impatient now.

Deva was out of the kitchen now. Standing in a completely different light and posture.

"It takes courage to fight injustice, Neel Baba. There are always moments of uncertainty, fear, self-doubt. We all have been bullied throughout our childhood and youth. We understand how it works and how it feels. Courage is not a state of mind. It is a response. It happens in a split second. It is either acceptance or standing up to the bully. Bravery is not a habit; it is merely an event."

Neel had his mouth gaping open. It was Deva talking. His sweet teddy bear, Deva.

Amma was serious now.

"We derived our courage from our team. Our cricket team. Our team was our country's response to the world that we would not be bullied any more. We, as a formerly bullied nation, stood up and fought back. Our team taught the whole country not to take it lying down. Our team was telling all of us that we would fight and decimate anything that was stopping us. Cricket became a vehicle for justice. Every date of extraordinary achievement by our team became a symbol, a beacon for justice. It gave us the courage and strength to commemorate and immortalise those dates in our own lives. By taking a stand. By eliminating evil. Hence, those dates, and what better medium is there to carry out this honourable quest than the cricket kit itself? So it was either the bat or ball."

Amma was fluently describing something that was life-changing for him. For them.

"Also, a cricket bat was obvious, but who would suspect a ball, right? I mean, what can one ball do? When they are together in a bunch, they can be formidable weapons and cave in the skull of a bastard who had it coming." completed Ibu.

Neel had to take a moment to take this all in. But he had more questions.

"So, you guys celebrated every Indian cricketing milestone by eliminating one culprit by bashing his skull with a dozen cricket balls. Repeatedly. I mean…but the strength required to do that… I mean, no offence, but….you guys…" Neel was right.

"Balraam Pandit. Of course, it was the Hulk…Balli uncle." Neel answered his own question.

"Were you able to establish that, by the way, Neel?"

"Yes, Ibu… eventually. The balls were always deformed and askew. There was no plausible explanation for that. And when I got the hunch, I requested Kaka to check for the residue of the lacquer, sheen or the seam thread of a cricket ball on the blood-stained wig of Eknath Patil… and….it came out positive."

"Bravo…that was really brilliant, Neel …" Amma was genuinely proud.

"Ok, but all of this requires so much work…the surveillance, the blind spots, the surety of not leaving any evidence, the technology and skill required here… I mean… how?"

Amma and Ibu looked at each other but kept quiet.

"It had to be someone younger, someone tech-savvy, someone who shares your ideas and views and someone close enough……of course……" Neel had a moment.

"It was Asif, of course… the suave….smart…Asif. Even the CCTV footage of your absence from the bar could be doctored if need be.......Wow!!!!" Neel was genuinely impressed now.

Deva came with a glass of water and Neel's medicine. Neel looked at Deva a little differently and dutifully took it. Deva patted Neel's head lovingly and said, "Neel Baba...I know you. You would have done the exact same thing. I know in my heart. I know you." And then he left with Neel lost in the words he had just uttered.

"What was the final confirmation for you, Neel?"

"Mhatre. Sub-inspector Mhatre. I asked him to find the guest list for that night. All the details from that night's party. The attendance, the employees that night, everything. It took him a day and a half, but he sent it across. And then it was....a bit clear. All the names were there..."

"Well, there you have it." Amma made a gesture to get up.

"What now?" Neel's voice boomed.

The 2 septuagenarians looked at him quizzically.

"What happens now? Amma...Ibu...Deva... what now?"

"Ramesh Chavan will die. He has to. Soon." Deva said it aloud from the kitchen.

Amma stood and stretched himself a bit.

"The monster... has been contained for now. In fact, he will actually live in fear for the time being. He has been threatened and neutralised by certain means, which we initially didn't approve, but we had to do it. When it comes to Chavan and what he is capable of, he needs to be caged at any cost. That cockroach Gadhvi helped a little. I mean, he was at least involved in a noble cause. His death was worth way more than his life. The number 6.........So....Chavan will die slowly. A little every day....looking over his shoulder. He deserves to live in constant fear. Let him be sleepless and restless and wait for an ultimate blow. He can live in hell for now. But he will be eliminated eventually. ***Antatogatva.***" Amma announced with an air of finality.

It was already afternoon, and they had to take their before-meal medication. Both of them took their meds and casually went out to the terrace for some fresh air.

Neel was a little baffled at this abrupt ending and was left standing exasperated right in the middle of dining area.

"So, what do we eat tonight, Deva? What are the specials for tonight to celebrate this iconic day?" Amma shouted from outside.

"Mutton Pulao, Shiksha will make," Deva replied from inside the kitchen.

And a befuddled Neel was standing in the middle. He ventured out.

"Amma…Ibu….what…. so we pretend nothing has happened? Is that it? That's it?"

"Neel…we made a choice. It was ours. We can't make one for you. You have to do it yourself. We will support you in whatever you want to do. Simple."

Neel was standing over the 2 gentlemen sitting on the settee.

"And what will you guys do now?" he asked.

"We are going to watch the Indian Team make history tonight." Came the reply almost in unison.

47

NOVEMBER 19ᵀᴴ, 2023

Clarence House, 10:00 PM

It was not meant to be. Gods were cruel tonight. There was a dead silence on the semi-covered terrace of Clarence House. Nobody was eating or drinking anymore. They were in mourning. The nation was in mourning. It was the usual group on a usual match night riddled with unusual expressions due to an unusual result. Amma broke the silence. Someone had to.

"Well, you win some. You lose some. But I am proud of our boys. What a campaign. They have inspired the future generation for years to come. To our boys!!!" Amma raised his glass.

"Hear hear, to our boys!" The group echoed.

"Alright, how about some mutton pulao to elevate the spirits, huh?" Shiksha threw the question on the table.

"Umm…I need one more drink before that." Amma announced, and Ibu joined in. And just like that, people got up, dusted themselves off, and normalcy returned. A bit.

After the sumptuous meal, they were all chatting away the blues. Suddenly, Kamble sat upright and asked.

"Say, Neel, what about that forensic analysis, huh? It came positive yaar. What about it? That was a long shot. I mean, what made you even think in that direction? What did you conclude?"

There was a pin-drop silence, and all eyes were on Neel now.

"It was a dead end, Kaka. I mean, I had a hunch, which was confirmed, but the facts don't support it. Plus, I warmed up to Gadhvi's death as an accident. I had a confirmation bias. All facts point to the Colonel doing it. But whoever attacked us in Alibaug is still out there, so my investigation remains open......"

Kamble didn't believe a word of it. Of course, Neel was lying through his teeth. But he was too tired and too bruised to care.

"Okay... that was....unusual...Neel Mantri. You are hiding... or...stalling... or...I don't know. But you are growing, and that is much I can see and vouch for."

Kamble turned to Amma and clasped his hand in his palm.

"Amma, I have seen this boy think logically and deeply. His biggest learning in this case was that sometimes you have to get out of your own way. If he does that consistently, he does have a future in detection. He is indeed, dare I say, a Sherlock or Feluda. And in this case..."

Kamble paused for a moment as if formulating and weighing what he was about to say.

"I think anyone who tried to eliminate us just for being there in Alibaug is a cruel monster with no moral compass. It could be Chavan or somebody else ...I don't know yet. But I have a strong feeling that all the victims in this case....had it coming... It was all about ...justice."

Neel stood up and went up to the terrace, staring at the sky.

"I agree, Kaka. There has to be justice here in this world. I am convinced that someone can be killed for the right reasons. I am convinced that there is definitely a rightful termination of life."